White Friday

Ray Jordan

Copyright © 2013 Ray Jordan

All rights reserved.

ISBN: 1492943762
ISBN-13: 978-1492943761

ACKNOWLEDGMENTS

I'd like to thank God.

Many thanks to Cassie Hanson for helping me stay sane... assuming I was to begin with.

Also I'd like to thank Wayne Wolfe, Annie Grier Rowan, and a few other people who prefer to remain anonymous.

Finally, I'd like to distance myself from some of the crude things that my characters say and do. They do not reflect me personally.
-R.J.

PROLOGUE
NOVEMBER 13TH

Glenn Wallace had just entered the dorm stairwell when he heard a feminine squeal and a THUMP from somewhere above. Undergrads, most likely, fooling around. The perils of putting graduate students and undergraduates in the same building. Those "kids" were always doing something immature. Glenn should know; he had been one of them until six months ago. Fortunately, he had graduated.

He started up the stairs, hoping that he wouldn't have to pass by (and ignore) some painfully childish courtship display. Then he heard the hit.

Glenn had heard that sound before. On his third day of junior high—just when he was starting to get used to the place—a fight had broken out between two foul-tempered boys. From what he could tell, one of the boys, Stephen, had a fairly stable home life—his mother picked him up every day, his clothes were of decent quality and he was generally well-equipped for school. In fact, Glenn could never figure out why Stephen had been so foul-tempered. The other boy, James, however... his clothes didn't always fit him properly, and sometimes they were wrinkled, worn out or stained. He usually spent his lunch period bumming food off the people around him. After school, he would often be seen walking around aimlessly, or sauntering down an alley with older troublemakers. James probably had some reasons to be unhappy. But whatever the reason, these two boys wound up fighting near Glenn's locker. The first blow came when James' clenched fist smashed into Stephen's cheekbone with a surprisingly low-key THWAP sound. Not the thunder-crack punching sound of a movie hero, but the frighteningly real sound of a fist causing damage to a skull.

That was the sound Glenn heard in the stairwell. It was followed by another feminine squeal, this one more insistent.

Glenn froze. His brain was locked up. He couldn't think.

He looked up. Three floors above. *Am I the only one hearing this??*

Now a coarse male voice echoed down from above: "Quit making me do this."

Silence, except for perhaps a faint whimpering. Then a decisive SLAP and the male voice: "Stop it! Where is he?!"

The whimpering grew louder.

Glenn didn't know it, but all of his muscles were tensed. His mind was so focused on the sounds that he couldn't see a thing; his eyesight had effectively disconnected. He wanted very much to turn around and leave. Walk back toward the classroom buildings, maybe sit in the library for a while and forget all of this. He definitely didn't want to hear any more.

His brain caught up with him at the landing between the second and third floors. He was taking the steps two at a time. No one on the second floor landing, no one on the third floor—

Another THWAP, and a gasp.

As Glenn climbed the final half-flight of stairs to the fourth floor, he saw the back of the man—coated in denim and wool. Scruffy and lanky. Leaning over someone who was seated in the corner of the landing. He was shouting now, blocking out the sobbing of his victim. "I AIN'T GONNA STOP! WHERE IS HE?! WHERE IS HE?!" He landed another blow.

Glenn, gasping for breath now, reached the landing and closed the gap quickly. He grabbed Scruffy man's arms from behind, swung him around and shoved him toward the stairs. Scruff stumbled down a few steps before regaining his balance. He glared up at Glenn, shocked and angry. "Hey!"

Glenn didn't respond. He was staring at Scruff's terrified victim.

1
NOVEMBER 27TH... Today

The hamper sat in the corner of Glenn's bedroom. It was collapsible—polyester mesh supported by a flexible wire frame, with two woven handles on top and even a side pouch for a box of fabric softener. Clothes went into it only when they were legitimately smelly-dirty or stained. A t-shirt worn only to one class or a pair of jeans worn only for a few days would not qualify. Only when the hamper was full, and sometimes only when it reached "heaping" status, would there be a trip to the laundry room. And today, the hamper was about two-thirds of the way full. However, Glenn's comforter hadn't been washed since his mom bought it for him in mid-August, and he had to admit, it was starting to smell a little gamey.

Glenn folded the thick navy blue comforter, rolled it up and stuffed it into the hamper as far as it would go. He looked at his twin-sized bed and the Batman sheets. They could probably use a washing as well, but one step at a time. He didn't believe in shopping on the day after Thanksgiving, but it felt right to do *something* productive.

Despite having worked in a department store during the holiday season one year, he had never grasped the intended meaning of the term "Black Friday." Glenn had always disliked that day and the compulsive shoppers that it brought out, so, to him, "Black Friday" came to mean "a Friday of gloom or dread." If at all possible, he would stay at home on that day.

A good worker, but not the most conventional one, Glenn had decided, around eleven o'clock on Wednesday night, to start his two short (five page) papers that were due on Monday. He eventually got into such a groove that he didn't feel like stopping... at least, until the sun came up on Thanksgiving Day and he could no longer keep his eyes open. One paper was finished and the other over half done, so he felt fine taking a nice long rest. It wasn't until around one-thirty in the afternoon when, looking for "breakfast," he realized he had completely missed the Thanksgiving Day parade, quite possibly his favorite parade ever. But, hey, at least there was still football.

Glenn turned toward the full-length mirror next to the closet and looked at himself. Just short of six feet tall, sturdy with good shoulders. Yes, he had taken on some weight since graduating high school, but perhaps that was to be expected after quitting football. Glenn could still remember the day when he had discovered that a thirty-four inch waist would no longer accommodate him. That discovery had distressed him at first, but he had come to terms with it. *I carry it well*, he constantly told himself. *The broad shoulders make the weight less noticeable.* And it wasn't entirely denial, which made it even easier to accept. He had strong enough facial features to be considered functionally handsome, and a healthy head of brown hair. Nothing special there, just brown. There had been a reddish tint once, but it disappeared during his toddler years. His hair had almost been shaggy, but he had recently trimmed it down to a quarter-inch length with his roommate's clippers and a little assistance.

Craig, the roomie, had inspired the haircut with a similar one of his own. Glenn's hair hadn't been that short since, well, shortly after high school. Football had been good for him, at the very least, in keeping him disciplined. These days, only classes and his twenty hours a week working at the drug store kept him on a regular schedule. Yes, he spent around fifteen hours a week on schoolwork, but he could do that at any time as long as he met deadlines. When Craig wasn't available to hang out, Glenn generally spent his remaining time lounging around, watching TV and, rarely, reading for leisure. One of his more nebulous aspirations involved writing a novel, or perhaps a series of novels. School and work, however, consistently sapped his work ethic, and he couldn't think of a good story anyway.

Glenn changed out of his pajama pants and into a good old pair of worn-in carpenter jeans, topped off with a yellow football t-shirt. He gathered up his quarters, counting eleven in all. That would pay for two loads. He picked up the hamper and the bright orange detergent bottle and looked around. His bedroom, like all of them, was nothing special—16' by 12', beige walls and a mottled tan and brown carpet. The standardized wooden dorm furniture was unremarkable, but sturdy enough to endure constant student use. There was a desk and a plain chair, a five-foot dresser and a creaky single bed. Opposite the door was a tall window covered by wide horizontal blinds. They had remained closed for almost the entire semester.

He surveyed the room, trying to overcome a vague feeling that he often got when leaving: a feeling that he might, possibly, be forgetting something. Dirty clothes, check. Detergent, check. Quarters, check. Apartment key, check. Pants... check. At the last moment, he grabbed his cell phone, an almost two year-old model, just in case. Beside the bedroom was a rather spacious bathroom, as in every suite, and a very short hallway led to the common area—kitchen, living room, dining area and foyer—with the other bedroom and bath on the opposite end. In all, the common area was about the size of four bedrooms, with large front windows looking out toward the parking lot.

Although, Glenn supposed, this building was technically a dorm, it looked more like a respectable hotel than typical student housing. Inside, it had the same spackled beige walls and carpeting everywhere—although the colors in the carpet were slightly different on each floor. The "twin dorms," as they were known, had been built in 1991 and named after two of Tomlin University's particularly outstanding donors. Glenn lived in Jackson Hall. Its twin brother across the parking lot was Wallace Hall—no relation to him. They were much nicer than the other four dorms scattered about the campus, and they packed in fewer students, only about one hundred each. The other, older dorms housed nearly twice as many students in about the same square footage, so those folks randomly selected for the twin dorms felt quite lucky indeed. Spacious suites, a separate bathroom and shower for each person... one could say that residents of the twin dorms were spoiled. They might even be right. Glenn and Craig lived on Jackson's third floor in the east wing, closest to the elevators and stairwell at the center of the building. It was shaped, basically, like a big letter 'E.' Two hallways turned out from the main hall at right angles, with a stairwell and an exit at the end of each. Those outer halls featured the single apartments, whereas the two-bedroom suites made up the backbone of the building. The main entrances were at the middle of the main section—with a rather spacious lobby in the front and the main stairwell in the back. That back entrance, into the stairwell, which Glenn had used on that shocking afternoon two weeks ago.

He used the main stairwell now, so he could look out the windows at the landings between each floor. Something outside had caught his eye as he passed through the common area of his suite, and here he paused to look at it again. The 10' by 10' window was divided into panes about two square feet in size, looking out the back of the building toward the main part of campus. There he could see a small pond, then the broad Communications building and beyond, the proud gymnasium. An imposing blanket of clouds filled the sky, but more importantly... it was snowing. Snowing with purpose. Big, hearty-looking flakes, not just drifting down, but driving themselves to the ground in droves. This was an invasion of snow.

He had seen it coming down last night as well, but not quite with the same ferocity. Apparently, it had not stopped during the interim, because the world through the window was covered in white. The first snow of the season and, yes, he was impressed. It could even turn out to be the largest single snowfall of all his time here in Hagerstown. Though time would tell if it could match the output of Buffalo, New York. Somehow, he doubted it.

The laundry room was located on the first floor of the west wing, at the bend in the hallway. Glenn didn't encounter a soul on his way down, nor did he hear any sounds, not even his own footsteps. He felt extremely comfortable walking through this large, carpeted building in his socks. It was largely private; only residents could enter, by swiping their student identification cards at the door. And even during a regular school week, it was unusual to see more than one or two other people while moving through the building. Sometimes he legitimately felt like he had the whole place to himself. Home, Glenn decided, was where you could do everything in your socks.

This week, of course, the student population had dwindled to almost nothing. Classes went on normally, for the most part, until Wednesday. On the Monday of a week like this, eighty percent of students might show up for their classes. On Tuesday, closer to sixty percent. Wednesday, maybe half... but probably not. The lure of Thanksgiving break... or *any* holiday break... was just too strong. Since Wednesday morning, Glenn had seen only one other person in the building. He couldn't guess as to how many had elected to spend the holiday here in the dorm... but he was sure there weren't many. He had done it four... no, five years in a row now. Driving back to Buffalo took too long and flying cost too much. He would drive back home for Christmas, always.

He stepped into the laundry room, feeling the cold tile floor through his socks, and surveyed the place. Shockingly, it looked the same as it had on each of his two hundred or so trips down here. Five top-loading washing machines along one wall, each with a small digital display, all blank at the moment. Along the adjacent wall, a long table. Across the room, facing the washers were six dryers, stacked two high. A few feet away from those, a humming soda machine and a change machine. An empty white laundry basket (and a discarded plastic water bottle) sat on the floor next to the table, and all the washing machine doors were open except the one in the middle. Out of sheer curiosity, Glenn looked inside and, after a few seconds, recognized that the soggy clothing inside belonged to a girl. He closed the lid immediately out of respect; he didn't feel like looking at a woman's underwear without her permission. That was something that had to be earned, and it was worth being earned. He knew from experience.

So, he stuffed his comforter into the fifth machine. It

White Friday

fit, with no room to spare, and Glenn made a little impressed "hmm" to himself. Into the fourth machine he tossed all of his colored clothes. The remaining pile of whites was small, mostly just socks and a couple of white t-shirts. No need to spend another $1.25 on that; he'd wait until next week when the pile had doubled in size. He turned to pick up the detergent bottle and caught a glimpse of the soda machine. Damn, that bottle pictured on the front, covered in enlarged beads of water, made him thirsty. Glenn loved soda, but made an effort to avoid buying it regularly. As much as he believed... about eighty percent of the time... that he looked fine with a little extra weight, constant soda-drinking would only add to it, and he certainly didn't want that. Some of his family members drank it like it was water, which just seemed wrong. But, as a treat now and then, soda was fine.

It had actually been... yes, over a week, since he'd had any soda. Glenn decided that he was due. He strolled over to the machine, still admiring the photograph printed on the front. The price for a bottle: $1.25. Glenn had eleven quarters. Math had never been the easiest subject for him, but there was an obvious dilemma here.

Clearly one load of laundry would have to wait. He touched the comforter and said "I'm sorry, just be patient." He poured some detergent in with the colors, inserted the required five quarters and started the machine. Five more quarters went into the soda machine, and a bottle of bright green liquid tumbled out. Not dripping with water as the picture suggested; perhaps the machine was malfunctioning. It was gloriously cold, though. Glenn took a swallow of it and his mouth rejoiced. The carbonated bubbles and the sweetness—it was addictive.

He decided to take the easy way back to the third floor—let the elevator fight gravity for him. He pressed the UP button and took another swig of soda while looking around the lobby. It was about the size of a suite's common area but, aside from a couple chairs and an unremarkable potted plant, pretty much empty. The wall across from the elevators contained about a hundred mailboxes. And out through the double-doors, he could see the snow, still falling, in the dull afternoon light.

Glenn felt comfortable and secure here, but seeing the snow falling made him feel a tug—just a little tug, yes—toward the place where he had spent the first eighteen years of his life. Toward mom and dad and the warm, loving glow of home. Without even thinking, he took a few steps toward the doors, reaching into his pocket for his phone. He heard one of the elevators opening, but getting upstairs had become less of a priority.

Still approaching the front doors, he pulled out his phone, dialed an area code and a few more numbers. The phone automatically completed the number for him, saved in its memory—the one entitled "Home." He pressed the "dial" button.

An awning extended over the sidewalk, covering the width of the entrance. For the most part, that area had been shielded from snow. Glenn opened one door and stepped out as he put the phone to his ear. Needless to say, the sidewalk was much colder than the laundry room floor. Armies of snowflakes continued to dive-bomb the ground resulting in, so far, almost two feet of snow. No roads within sight had been plowed. He knew where the sun would be, low in the sky to the right, although he could hardly see any indication of it through the dense clouds. Across the parking lot, about a hundred yards away, was the twin of this building, a mirror image, like two horseshoe magnets just barely held apart.

During the third ring, he heard his mother's voice: "Hello?"

"Hi, mom." He stepped back into the building. Over the

phone came music from the ever-present radio station—oldies, of course. Through morning, afternoon and dinner time, the likes of Frank Sinatra, Glenn Campbell, Simon & Garfunkel and the like filled the Wallace home. Generally, any easygoing music from between the years of 1950 and 1980. He hadn't always enjoyed it, but over time it had become one of the comforting aspects of home, like the overstuffed easy chairs and the jar filled with chocolate peanut butter cups throughout the fall.

"Heyyy! It's the boy," she said happily, loud enough to ensure that dad, who was likely nearby, heard it as well. "What are you doing?"

"I'm just about to wash my comforter. I thought I should tell you."

"For the first time?"

"Yeah. I didn't think it would fit in the machine. But it does."

"Well, that's great. How often do you wash your sheets?"

He sighed. "I don't know... I'll probably do those next."

"You should," said mom in her smooth and sociable way. Her *I'm glad to hear from you* way. "So you had a good Thanksgiving?"

He shrugged. "It was okay. I had a pretty good turkey pot pie..."

"Who made that?"

He stared into space for a few moments. A few feet past the awning, where the road was, someone had made a snow angel. Someone relatively short. He realized that he knew who had made it. "It came from the store," he said slowly. "It was... good." Technically it was true; the *ingredients* had all come from the store.

"I can make a pot pie, next time you come home."

"Sure. Christmas."

"I know. I'll be ready. Did you get any good deals today?"

He had to stop and think for a moment. "I don't shop on Black Friday."

"I did. JC Penney opened at six. There were a lot of people there."

Glenn shook his head. "You don't get up that early after a food-based holiday. It's just not practical."

"Your dad slept in until eight o'clock."

"Wow..."

"Oh, I saw Mrs. Patterson at the store... you know, Tara's mother?"

"Oh. Yeah...?"

"She was a year behind you, right? Didn't you like her?"

Glenn sighed. He might have liked her for a while in high school. She had been a smart, self-sufficient girl, a track star who, unfortunately, didn't feel the need for a boyfriend. That fact alone made her special. And it made Glenn want her even more. To no avail. "I'm sure I did," he said.

"I asked her mom if she has a boyfriend..."

"Mom, please, don't."

"Well, when are you going to start looking for a girl?"

"I'll be fine. There are plenty of girls around here. It is a co-ed dorm, you know."

"Any nice ones?"

"Yes. Okay?"

A silent moment and then: "Okay. I guess I have to trust you."

"Yeah." Glenn was ready to move on. He walked back toward the elevator and pressed the UP button again. It opened almost immediately.

Someone was in the elevator. Lying on the floor, in the corner, as if taking a nap. A girl, petite but not without curves, wearing faded jeans and a red hooded sweatshirt that said "ALABAMA" on the front. Dark-ish golden hair, slightly past shoulder-length, tied back. There was an adorable childlike quality to her face, even with closed eyes and no expression. It was Ashley.

Glenn stared at her for several seconds. His brain had frozen up. Mom was talking again, but it was just white noise in his ear. "Mom," he said finally. "I have to go."

"What? Why?"

"Something's... come up. I'll call you later."

"Okay... Be safe."

Glenn ended the call and dropped the phone into his pocket. "Ashley."

Ashley didn't move. She looked like she had curled up to keep herself warm. Or else, in pain. There was nothing visibly wrong with her... she may have looked a little pale, but that could have been from the elevator lights.

As he stared, the elevator door began to close. He frantically stuck a hand in front of it, triggering the sensor. The door slid open again.

"Ashley. Ashley." She wasn't moving. He looked closer, concentrating on her midsection... there was no breathing. Glenn didn't know how to perform CPR, but... from the looks of it... CPR wouldn't help.

The soda bottle plopped to the floor and bounced. Shaken, he reached down for it, grabbing at air a couple times before his hand finally found it. Instinctively, he opened the cap, wanting a drink. The fizzing soda overflowed, ran down over his hand and dripped on the floor. Normally that would have angered him, but here... it somehow made the situation real.

He stepped into the elevator just far enough to push the "lock" button so the door wouldn't close again. Ashley looked... diminished somehow. Not physically smaller, but it seemed like there was just... less to her than before. Almost as if someone had been wearing an Ashley suit, then had taken it off and tossed it on the floor. A pillow with the stuffing taken out. This wasn't Ashley... this was Ashley's body.

"I'm sorry, sir, but we may not be able to get to you as soon as we'd like. The weather conditions are extending our response time."

"O...kay," Glenn replied unsteadily. The 911 operator sounded a little like his mother. That didn't help things.

"You said there's no one in immediate danger, correct?"

"Not that I know of..."

"If that's the case, it could take up to two hours."

"Wow. Okay."

"Can we reach you at this number?"

"Yeah."

"And your name, sir?"

"Glenn... Wallace."

"Can you give me your room number?"

"301."

"Okay, Glenn, thank you. What I need you to do is make sure no one moves the body. All right?"

"Well... yeah. It's just... I'm afraid someone's going to see her and... and freak out."

"Do you have something you can cover her with? A blanket perhaps?"

Glenn tried to think, to no avail. "Yeah... I'm sure I do..."

"Okay. Just make sure the body is not disturbed, do not attempt to clean the area around her as it could be a crime scene... and try to keep this line open, just in case. Help will be there as soon as possible."

Glenn put away his phone and tried to think. It was proving to be more difficult than usual. For a few minutes he just stood there, mired in a mental fog, watching the snowflakes fall.

Make sure no one moves the body.

But... someone's going to see her.

It could be a crime scene. You might disturb evidence.

But she's right there in the elevator! People use that!
You need to listen to the lady on the phone.
But if someone sees her, they'll panic or something!
Or something.
She was lying there, in a public area, helpless. He knew that it wasn't technically Ashley lying there, just the body she had left behind, but still, he had to do something. She deserved better than to be seen like that. She deserved to be remembered for the way she treated people when she was alive. Not as a body lying in the elevator. Ashley had gone where Glenn couldn't follow... not right now, anyway. But he could at least try to preserve her dignity here on earth.

Do you have something you can cover her with?

His mind was replaying the walk to the laundry room. Apparently it knew the answer before he did. He saw the door with the window in it, saw the washing machines... the one on the end with the open lid and... the navy blue comforter inside.

It was in the laundry room, halfway across the building. He wasn't about to leave her here while he went for it. Even if he ran there and back, he wouldn't feel comfortable leaving her body alone for that long. This almost felt like... kind of an intimate situation. Something shared between two people who trusted each other. *It's just between you and me, Ash. I won't leave you alone.*

He had checked for a pulse before making the phone call. Glenn was rarely squeamish; he had gutted fish and once helped a friend skin a deer. He had also seen a moderate number of football injuries, including a few on himself. But never before had he seen or touched a lifeless human body. There were funeral viewings, of course, but it was just different. A body at a viewing looked... prepared. The undertaker did what they could to make that person look like they were at peace. That was the deceased at their best. Sometimes they even ended up looking like mannequins. This, however, was fresh and raw and real. And it was random. Someone he had seen fairly regularly, who had lived just down the hall from him... whose cooking he had enjoyed on more than one occasion... was now lying on the floor, unresponsive.

Someone he had wanted to get closer to. Someone he had wanted to hold hands with. Someone he had wanted to kiss. It couldn't have been just a random acquaintance, could it?

He knelt beside the body and fumbled around nervously for a bit, not unlike an inexperienced teenager trying to get to second or perhaps even third base. Finally he got his arms around her in a good position and slowly stood. Ashley had stood just over five feet and weighed... well, over a hundred pounds... probably around one-twenty. That's a lot for anyone to lift, save a bodybuilder, and the limpness of the body just made it more difficult to control.

Glenn was strong enough to carry her down the hall to the laundry room without too much difficulty, walking as quickly as possible to avoid being seen. She wasn't noticeably cold, but there didn't seem to be any body heat, either. He set her down under the laundry table, arranged her in a fetal position and wrapped the comforter over her. If anyone did come in here over the next two hours, hopefully they'd take it for a pile of clothes.

Only after he had covered her up did the thought occur to him: *the police are going to be pissed.*

Oh well.

Glenn stood and looked at the huddled form on the floor. He felt weak and braced himself against the table for a minute. He choked out some words: "I'm sorry, Ashley. I'm sorry... for... *everything.*" "Everything" being the biggest word he could find to describe what she'd been through. Because, for her, everything could have been better. Everything.

How could this have happened?

As Glenn was hefting Ashley's lifeless form, a tall, skinny young man named Eric was collapsing backward onto a bed in a darkened room. His girlfriend had just done *the* most amazing thing with her mouth, and he felt as if his body and mind were both melting in ecstasy. He shuddered with pleasure and tried to catch his breath. Refractory period be damned...

His girlfriend sat up. It was a few seconds before she could speak. "I bet Samantha couldn't do that," she said thickly.

"Oh, come on," he said between mouthfuls of air. "We didn't even..."

"Didn't what?"

"No, never mind."

"You didn't make love?"

Silence.

"No, that can't possibly be it," she said.

"No, it's true," he sighed. "We just... thought we should... wait..."

"Seriously? You're kidding me."

"I'm not."

She let out a terse laugh and laid down beside him. "Too bad, hon. She seems like such a saucy little minx..."

"Let it go, please."

"Hey, it's not my problem. It's hers. She's going to regret letting you go."

He had caught his breath now. "You mean like, living well is the best revenge?"

She rolled up against him and wrapped an arm around his chest. "I don't know what you're talking about, dear... but revenge is about making other people miserable...

and she will be."
  "Wait... what?"

2

The walk from the laundry room back to the elevator seemed to take forever. Today had changed, from a possibly interesting, relaxing day off into something frightening. Glenn suddenly felt very isolated... in a bad way. But at the same time, he wasn't sure if he could feel comfortable around anyone at this point. He just didn't feel comfortable... at all.

Many people would have panicked upon finding the lifeless body of someone they had known. Glenn had never panicked in his life, and the possibility had never occurred to him. He had never been in a life-or-death situation before, but in times of heightened stress or fear, his mind actually seemed to... slow down. Whether this served as an advantage or not, he couldn't know. He had never really thought about it. He had, however, wondered why many of the people around him seemed so eager to "freak out" whenever the smallest things went wrong. On the other hand, the people who "freaked out" often wondered why Glenn appeared so apathetic.

He stepped into the elevator, unlocked it and sent it

up. As the doors closed he started to wonder... could there be evidence on the floor? She had been lying there for... a little while, at least. He crouched in the corner, setting down his soda and poking around on the floor. His shadow from the overhead lights got in the way, though, so he shifted to one side, just in time to notice the doors opening again. At the second floor. And feet—yes, those were definitely feet, standing outside the door. Someone with skinny, hairy legs and a decent tan still, wearing khaki shorts that extended down past the knee. On the feet were the kind of comfortable, lightweight walking shoes that would provide no protection whatsoever.

Glenn didn't have time to get up before the doors had opened and Eric had stepped in. Eric Carpenter, education major extraordinaire. Glenn had heard, from more than one source, that the people who didn't know what they wanted to do with their lives often majored in education. Eric stood an inch or two over six feet, skinny but not really athletic, with messy light-brown hair that was already starting to thin. He had a face that women seemed to consider "cute"... sort of long and unrefined with boyish features and a bashful smile. The kind of face that's almost too feminine for a man, but still too masculine for a woman. A brown corduroy satchel accompanied him wherever he went. He lived on the third floor as well, in one of the single apartments.

The doors were closing and, moments later, the elevator would continue upward. "Did you lose something?" Eric said as a greeting.

Glenn, still crouching, glanced around, uneasy. Trying to think, still. "Just a coin." Instantly he knew that was a pathetic attempt at a lie, but he couldn't say exactly why.

Eric looked amused. "Any specific kind of coin?"

Okay. Glenn decided to quit while he was behind. "I'm not picky," he said wearily as he stood. That drew a short laugh from Eric and Glenn chuckled a bit, hoping to diffuse the tension he felt. He was probably the only one who felt it. "Were you hanging out in the lounge?" The second-floor lounge was a suite-sized room right above the foyer, equipped with multiple sofas and chairs. People rarely used it.

"No, I was just with Sasha."

Glenn had to process that for a moment. "Oh, right, you're... dating." She lived in a second-floor suite. Glenn had not realized that either of them were spending their holiday weekend on campus.

Eric nodded primly. "Spent the night there. We just... started getting on each other's nerves."

Glenn nodded, pretending to understand. He didn't know Eric very well, but he could imagine him getting on people's nerves. That ever-casual attitude of his and the way he always seemed overly satisfied with himself... those kind of things annoyed him. Then there was the fact that Eric never stayed single for long. Nine times out of ten, it seemed, when Glenn saw Eric, the latter had a female with him. Sure, Glenn envied him. Glenn wanted a girlfriend more than anything. He wasn't desperate... he wouldn't go to extreme measures to get a girl... but when it came to females, they hardly ever seemed to give him any attention, and he just couldn't understand why. It came down to this: Eric was successful in that arena and Glenn was, largely, not. So, Glenn couldn't help but resent him.

That line of thought brought Ashley to mind. "I wonder who else stayed for the weekend," Glenn said, glancing at Eric.

Eric thought for a minute as the elevator door slid open. "Chuck, I think." He stepped out onto the third floor and Glenn followed. "Maybe Amy, not sure though..."

Glenn nodded absently. Chuck, a connoisseur of all things Japanese, had founded the small campus anime club. He lived on the fourth floor and stuck with a small group of enthusiastic friends which sometimes included Craig, for some reason. Amy was a pretty, outgoing overweight girl majoring in business administration. She had a take-no-shit attitude that Glenn found undeniably attractive. If not for Ashley, she might have been his favorite female on campus. She lived in a suite on the west side of the third floor.

"Oh, and Ashley," Eric added. "I saw her."

Glenn felt an inner shock at the mention of her name and he wasn't sure why. After a few moments he was able to speak. "When did you see her?"

Eric stopped just past Glenn's door and turned to face him. "Last night."

Glenn nodded, lost in thought as he pulled out his keys and unlocked the door. He assumed they had passed each other in the hall or something. Eric stood, watching him. "You know, she posted something online about liking a guy on her floor."

Glenn looked at the floor and made a "hmm" sound. He didn't feel like keeping up this conversation any longer, but he would never be so rude as to forcibly end it. Better to just let it die of starvation.

"*You're* on her floor," Eric said, giving the conversation a few needed morsels.

"So are you."

Eric gave a conspiratorial grin. "Right."

Glenn just shook his head, hoping the conversation would end there, and opened his door. Eric said nothing until Glenn was almost inside. "Mind if I hang out for a while?"

Glenn looked back at him for a moment, not sure what to say. "You mean, in here?"

Eric's friendly smile had a bit of a forced nature to it. "Yeah. Am I interrupting something?"

Glenn stared into space, not really seeing anything.

While he didn't feel like holding a conversation, the idea of company was not a complete turn-off. He actually missed his roommate. Craig was just about the only person he would have told about finding Ashley's body, but Craig was... somewhere, for the holiday. There was something uniquely comforting about having another human being around, even if you weren't constantly talking at each other. "No... I'm just doing laundry and... reading."

"Fun," said Eric.

Glenn continued into the suite, holding the door open for Eric to follow. Glenn walked past the dining area and leaned against the kitchen counter, watching to see what his guest would do. Eric took a few steps inside and looked around, presumably appraising the place, as the door swung itself shut. It looked like every other suite in the building. The living room came equipped with a small TV stand, a coffee table, two chairs and a couch—simple wooden constructions with decent cushions attached. In the dining area, near the door, stood a round wooden table and four chairs, duplicates of the simple one in the bedroom. The kitchen looked unremarkable; Glenn and Craig sometimes cooked rudimentary meals for themselves, but they cleaned up quickly and put their dishes away, always. Finally Eric sauntered into the living area, flopped down onto the couch and pulled out his laptop, a smallish but undeniably sleek Mac. "Craig went home for Thanksgiving?"

"He went somewhere. He wasn't very specific."

Eric smiled to himself as he uncoiled his laptop's power cable. "He's crazy, man."

Glenn smiled a little in turn. "You don't have to tell me." Crazy, yes... but in a weird way, also reliable. Interestingly, Craig was honest with Glenn even when withholding information. When speaking of his plans for Thanksgiving weekend, he'd said, "I'm not going to tell you where I'm going, but if something should go wrong and you need advice, just text." Craig worked as a Resident Assistant for the University Housing Department, his jurisdiction being, of course, Jackson Hall. He worked in the Housing Office a couple days a week, and a few set nights every week, he was on call for fellow residents with housing-related emergencies. About once a week, Glenn would see or hear his roommate pacing through the common area, trying to solve someone's problem over the phone. Always using humor, never showing frustration.

Glenn swung his arm toward Craig's closed bedroom door, as if to say, "thaaaat's Craig," but Eric was too busy plugging in his power cable to notice. Glenn thought for a moment. "Have you seen anyone else around? What about Sam?"

Eric didn't look up. "No. Haven't seen her for a while."

Glenn suddenly felt a bit awkward. "I just... assumed she'd be around."

"Probably across town with her family."

"Yeah. Are you two... still on... speaking terms?" He spent each pause searching for a way to say what he wanted to say, without saying it outright. It didn't help.

"Yeah, sure. It was, ya know, just about as mutual as a breakup can be."

Glenn, feeling a little more comfortable... "I heard some interesting things about you guys."

Eric finally looked up from his laptop, his face mostly hard. "Like what?"

"I heard you guys had... a lot of... uh... you know."

Eric stared. "Sangria?"

"Yes," said Glenn, after a moment of thought. "Yes."

"Only way I could get her to drink, with the fruit..."

Glenn thought for another moment. "Why was it so important that she drink?"

Eric stared into the air for a few moments. Then he

turned back to his laptop.

That had been a close call. The last thing Glenn wanted to do was to say what he had actually heard: a lot of *arguments*. He had assumed that Eric would have a sense of humor regarding his past mistakes... he should have known better than to assume.

The sudden end of their conversation left Glenn feeling awkward. He looked for his soda, craving a distraction more than anything else. It wasn't in the room. "Aw... crap," said Glenn.

Eric replied with a flat "Hmm?"

"My soda. I dunno where..." He looked around the suite cautiously, then at Eric. "You're good here?"

"Yeah, go ahead."

Glenn looked around one more time, subconsciously noting the positions of all the personal objects in the suite. Eric wasn't a complete stranger... just a scumbag. Not Glenn's first choice of company. Still, his desire to hang out seemed genuine enough. Perhaps he'd just had a fight with Sasha and didn't feel like being alone. After all, he rarely, if ever, saw Eric alone. It just so happened that Glenn was one of the few people around to hang with. He strongly doubted he would have been Eric's first choice, either. And that was just fine.

He took the stairs down to the first floor, working out some of the tension that had come up between the Ashley situation and the Eric situation. He felt weary and yet... energized at the same time. Amazing how quickly things can change, with the smallest impetus... a credit card... an essay requirement... a relationship status. A good day becomes a bad day. A relaxing vacation becomes a tense nightmare. White becomes black, or vice versa. A playing card may not seem like much, unless your house is made of them...

At that, he stopped and forced himself to think on more superficial things so that he wouldn't drown in the deep end of his own mind. He sure was thirsty... that greenish-yellowish soda, with its almost radioactive glow, would taste great right about now...

It was not in the first floor hall. It was not in the laundry room, either. But the blanket-covered shape remained under the table, as if he needed a reminder that he hadn't been dreaming or hallucinating when this day had suddenly turned crazy.

Eric waited thirty seconds... about thirty seconds; he didn't count... before slinking out of Glenn's suite and down the hall toward his own apartment. He stopped at the last door before the bend in the hallway—apartment 309. A suite. He knocked on the door with confidence. Sam was almost certainly still across town with her family—being spoiled further—so he didn't need to worry about bumping into her. Why pay to live on campus when her family owned a rather luxurious estate less than ten minutes away? Because they could afford to, he supposed. Eric had always held this opinion, even during their three-month relationship. He just hadn't brought it up because, well, he'd never had reason to. Yes. That's why. They had always gotten along very well, and they had been fun at parties, and they had made wonderful... sangria together. Until she finally decided to judge him: unworthy. And suddenly it didn't matter to her how well their personalities had clicked, or how much fun they'd had together, or how well that claret had complimented the raspberries...

She had wounded Eric, deeply. Usually *he* did the dumping. This way, it was so... unfair. Sure, if he lost interest in a girl after a few months and ended it, that was fine. That was justified. Being dumped... it didn't feel justified. But then, this was different! His previous relationships had been all about fun, thrills, and pleasure.

Flirting, and sex, and sleep! Or flirting, and alcohol, and sex, and sleep... or flirting, and dancing, and alcohol, and sex, and sleep... But after about one month of dating Sam, Eric had vaguely become aware of a change—he wasn't just having fun this time. He was building something. And he had wanted this something to grow stronger over time, and to last. Hell, after three months together, they hadn't even had sex yet. Not because they didn't feel the desire—they felt it very strongly. But Sam had brought up the possibility that sex can blind people in the beginnings of relationships, screw up their priorities, and Eric had actually... agreed. This hadn't kept them from pleasuring each other; they had never questioned that part—no one ever did. They just didn't "go all the way." And somehow Eric had felt closer to Sam than to any other girlfriend he could remember. Imagine that... becoming closer, getting to know each other better, by NOT having sex. By resisting their urges rather than immediately giving in to them. Just that one change—not a small one, but simple enough—had made quite a difference. They had talked. They had cuddled. They had laughed together over their sexual frustration. And, inexplicably, it was all good.

After she had dumped him, he had felt the desire to say nasty things about her, to anyone who would listen. Perhaps post some angry words online as well. He had resisted these urges... mostly... instead choosing to avoid and ignore her. While dating Sam, Eric had just assumed that she was the one member of her family who had managed not to become spoiled or entitled by her father's financial success. After being dumped, though, his thoughts began to drift into... darker places. He wouldn't let those thoughts control him, despite the way they popped up during his weaker moments. Still, the pain of her rejection had not yet disappeared. And while he could resist, for the most part, the bitterness, another emotion proved more difficult to manage: the desire to be close to someone. That's where Sasha came in.

She had come on to him in a way that made him feel like he was doing most of the work. Eric, in his hurt and lonely state, couldn't have possibly resisted. He had become attached to the feeling of lying curled up with someone special for hours, not worrying about sex or appearances, but just... being. Two people, together, being. He could not quite articulate this, but nonetheless, he could tell that Sasha would not understand. With her, it felt more like one of his old relationships. The physical intimacy was there; the emotional intimacy was not. They weren't building anything together. Yet, he still couldn't say no... he couldn't live without a woman's touch. In other words, he was a man.

It had been at least fifteen seconds since he'd knocked, and no answer. He stared blankly at the seasonal decoration hanging on the door: two cute, smiling scarecrows holding a wooden "welcome" sign. Ashley, Sam's roommate, had either bought that or made it. Knowing her, either was possible.

Eric looked around, ensured the halls were empty, and addressed the door: "Ashley? Hello?" He waited a few seconds, no answer. "Ashley, listen... if you're in there, I'm sorry." A few more seconds, still no response. "Sasha is sorry, too. She's just afraid to say so." He stood there for a moment, thinking. "I'll be at Glenn's place for a while if you want to talk."

He suddenly felt like having a beer. Or maybe something stronger.

Glenn found his soda after he had given up looking for it, sitting on the floor of the elevator. He picked it up and took a swig as the elevator ascended. Normally, this might have brightened his day slightly. Today, it simply kept his frustration at a low simmer.

The elevator didn't ascend very far, though. It had stopped after one floor and the doors slowly opened...

"Glenn!"

Sasha. She was like one of those long, impressive icicles you'll occasionally see in the heart of winter—long, skinny and dependably cool. There's something irresistibly beautiful, though, in the way it refracts the sunlight and in the smooth, undulating shape it takes as it slowly melts and hardens again, again, again. This was Sasha. Bright, resolute, penetrating. Her lips plump, her eyes excitable and sometimes downright ravenous. Sometimes they seemed too big for her face. Now was one of those times.

Her long, audaciously streaked hair fell over her shoulders, looking almost as if she had fluffed it mere moments ago. A tight tank top and a pair of booty shorts hugged her body... the outfit would have turned more heads if she'd had a little more meat on her bones, but she used what she had to her advantage, no doubt.

Glenn just looked at her, a little surprised. He had not expected to run into yet another person today.

"I was just coming to see you," she said with unnecessary enthusiasm.

Glenn didn't even think before responding, with similar energy, "Awesome! Why?"

Sasha put her hands against the door frame and leaned in, as if they were good friends. "I need computer help."

"Eric is around," Glenn said.

She tilted her head and smiled. "I heard that you once took a computer class."

As a matter of fact, he had... in high school. "It was an introduction to—"

"Come on, then!" She lunged forward and grabbed his wrist, pulling him toward the opposite hall.

Glenn didn't want to go along with her, but he went. He went because... well, look at her! He didn't always go for skinny chicks, but Sasha allured him; she had a gorgeous face and a general sultriness about her. It was difficult to look at her and not think *SEX*, given the way she dressed, made herself up, and even the way she positioned her long legs while seated. Most of the guys in the dorms felt the same way about her, even the ones who were ashamed to admit it. Her personality, however, grated on people. There were several guys (not to mention other girls) who would promptly leave the area when she appeared, whether in the dining hall, library, study lounges or at parties. She played the part of an effervescent, outgoing student like a valley girl on crack. That was about a third of the time. Otherwise, she was a sullen, withdrawn bitch. That seemed to drive away a lot of potential friends. The few that stuck around were sycophantic and shallow. Her boyfriends came and went at a rather brisk rate as well... assuming she even believed in monogamy. Glenn imagined that the sex was probably good, and frequent. He knew, however, that no amount of sex could keep a guy around indefinitely with a girl who obviously had significant personality problems.

"Eric knows nothing about computers?" Glenn asked.

"Nothing useful."

"Hey," said Glenn, thinking. "Have you seen Ashley lately?"

After a few moments, Sasha said, "Yeah. Why? Do you have a thing for her?"

Glenn debated for a few moments over whether to tell the truth or not. "Is it that obvious?"

She gave him one last tug, and they had arrived at room 206, halfway down the west hall. "Yeah. The question is, why?" She pulled her room key out of somewhere in her shorts, though they didn't appear to have pockets, and opened her door.

Glenn thought about the question as he followed her inside. His eyes flicked downward for a moment, admiring the tightness of the shorts over her ass. "She's just so... genuine," he answered honestly. He didn't respect Sasha, and he was pretty sure he didn't like her, but getting into her suite nonetheless felt like somewhat of an accomplishment. She may not have been well-liked, but she was quite well-known; in fact, those who hated her probably outnumbered those who simply knew him. *That's right... I've been in Sasha's place, who wants to touch me?*

The door swung shut, punctuating his thoughts. After a few steps, Sasha halted abruptly and Glenn walked right into her from behind. He quickly grabbed her around the waist so she wouldn't fall, feeling both awkward and aroused. They were the same height. Her... was perfectly level with his... and the contact was... stimulating. "Oops," she said with a giggle.

She had tricked him into touching her—he had no doubt. And he was okay with it.

She made no effort to pull away, and the thought of removing his hands from her waist did not occur to him. "It's in the bedroom," she said, turning her head to the left.

He could feel her hip bones. After a moment or two, he said, "Okay."

She finally pulled away and grabbed him again—this time by the hand—and led him to her bedroom. Glenn looked around the suite briefly, trying to think of something non-flesh-related. Some weak late-afternoon light leaked through the closed shades, but not enough to illuminate the place very well. He could vaguely make out the standard dining table and chairs, some shadowy furniture in the living area, and, unmistakably, a large flat-screen television on the wall. That might have brought a pang of envy, had his mind been functioning at normal speed. They passed the small kitchen, where the counters appeared to be covered with empty food containers and utensils, and Glenn slowly came to the conclusion that Sasha's hand was cold. Not that it mattered.

After a few steps into the bedroom, they stopped. She let go of his hand and backed toward the bed, eyes fixed on him. "What do you think?" she asked, looking expectant.

There were lights on in here, at least. It was a standard bedroom, like Glenn's. Enough room for comfort, and not much more—he liked to think of it in terms of a shoebox for a hamster. He saw that Sasha had deigned to use the standard bedroom furniture: desk, dresser, bed frame, although her mattress looked much thicker than the ones that came with the dorms. And instead of the bare-minimum wooden chair, a mobile, high-backed office chair. She had also added a small refrigerator at the foot of her bed, and another, smaller flat-screen television on the wall facing the bed. Pink dominated wherever possible—the decorations, the bed sheets, curtains and, in fact, the office chair. On the desk sat a large, sleek-looking laptop, originally white, but wearing some sort of pink covering.

"Interesting," said Glenn.

"Can I make you a drink?"

"I'm sure you can. The question is, may you?"

"You are so *smart*!" she exclaimed.

"I have…" He held up his soda.

"You have a *mixer*," she said, as if to a slow-learning student. She leaned forward and opened her bottom desk drawer—the deepest one. Glenn peeked inside—there were at least a dozen bottles of various liquors, none completely full. He met her eyes again with, he was sure, at least a little surprise in his face. "Come on, now," she said with an intimate smile. "I've heard even you like a beer every now and then."

He nodded briefly, looking away. That was true. Most of the residents drank at least occasionally. But he had never seen such a large supply of hard liquor on campus before. There were no regular searches or inspections of the dorms, but if maintenance or any other staff members visited a room and saw any indications of banned substances... there would be trouble. Glenn knew of a guy named Scott who had been forced to move out because maintenance people had seen an empty wine bottle in his bedroom—a prop for a theatre class. The Housing Department refused to consider any extenuating circumstances. Of course, it seemed that certain popular or well-known people, like Sasha, never got caught.

"I don't do beer," she was saying, "but how about scotch? That's a manly drink." Her eyes looked extra wild for the briefest of moments. Glenn searched them for a few seconds, then nodded. She snatched his soda from him, pulled a half-full bottle of brownish liquid from the drawer and turned toward the mini-fridge.

Glenn stood there for a moment, not sure what to think. His gaze drifted toward the desk. There was an orange prescription bottle near the back, its label turned toward the wall. Then he remembered the laptop. "What's the problem with this?" he asked, sitting down in the pink chair.

"The internet."

Okay then. Glenn had a functional knowledge of computers, not enough to perform complicated repairs, but usually enough to figure out common issues. He went straight to the network settings and saw that, obviously, the computer was not connected to the dorm's wireless network. He tried the normal connection process, because, well... sometimes that worked. Sasha probably knew full well, like most college students, how to connect to a wireless network at the very least. But Glenn liked to try the simple solutions first and avoid wasting time if at all possible. The computer seemed to spin its wheels for a few seconds and then... it connected. Glenn smiled to himself and his mind began to muse whimsically that the pink thing had just needed the proper touch. Then the wheels in his head began to spin. He hadn't actually fixed anything. Either there had been a network problem and it had resolved itself... or everything been working fine all along.

He was trying to think of another explanation when a glass full of gold-ish fizzing liquid appeared next to him, held gently by a slim hand with long, smooth fingers. The hand set down the glass near his, hovered for a moment, then decisively came to rest on top of his. The touch, unexpected, sent a shiver through his arm and down through his torso. The fingers intertwined themselves with his and he heard slow, soft breathing very near to his ear. Warmth close behind him, then her cheek pressed against the side of his head. Glenn was very sensitive to touch, and for this reason he avoided casual contact whenever possible. Aside from handshakes and the occasional hugs, he only ever touched women he was interested in, and even then, only when he thought they liked him as well. Now her other hand was sliding down his other arm. He couldn't think. *This is what having a stroke must feel like... if I'm not having one, that is.* He couldn't move; so many nerves were sending confused and excited reports to his brain that the lines simply must have been jammed.

Sasha pulled on his shoulder, swiveling the chair, and him, toward her. Within moments, their faces were inches apart. She slid the tip of her nose down across his cheek and their mouths, like magnets, simply came together. As if they had come into existence just for this—a hungry kiss, one that knew it was only a prelude to what would come.

Glenn had kissed a few girls, sure, and had gotten physical with a couple of them, but none of them had given him a sensory overload like this, sending his nerve endings screaming their overwhelmed (but happy) reports to his brain. Her hands were exploring now, slowly moving south, but occasionally doubling back to emphasize certain points. She knew exactly what to touch and how... no, none of the other girls had displayed expertise quite like this, at least not during their first kiss. He started moving his own hands around, caressing and squeezing everything he could find, prompting the occasional moan of approval. Her tongue was in his mouth suddenly, a surprise to him.

One of her hands reached down toward the southern hemisphere, where a potentially dangerous uprising had begun. She happily gave it her full support.

Her hands slowly found the hem of his shirt and began to pull it up. Glenn broke off the kiss, momentarily surprised... then he recovered and allowed her to pull it off. He didn't need an invitation to reciprocate; by the time his had landed by the door, he had hers halfway off. She affected an admiring smile as he pulled it over her head, flung it backwards out of sight, and reached around to unhook her bra. It was black and sheer, which disappointed him—he had expected pink. After what felt like a full minute of fumbling—probably around fifteen seconds, really—the bra came loose and he slipped it off. Her smile remained and she giggled a little as he appraised her torso. Then she took his hand and led him to her bed.

She turned his back to the bed and gave a playful shove—not enough to push him down, but he got the idea and went with it, falling backward. The bed that he hit was not the bed he expected; it rippled like a wave, as if... filled with water.

"You're kidding me," he said, half to himself. He hadn't seen a waterbed in at least a decade.

Sasha smiled and bit her lower lip. "It's amazingly fun once you know how to use it. I'll teach you." She crawled onto the bed, straddling him, then lowered herself onto him. Once again, there seemed to be some invisible force pulling their mouths together, and they met in another hungry kiss. Hips began to grind.

Glenn was no longer thinking, only feeling and reacting. It was all he could do at the moment. After two or three minutes of kissing and fondling, Sasha shifted her weight and moved onto the bed beside him. The waterbed undulated in response. She ran a hand down, down from his chest, following a natural southern trail. She reached denim and metal; she knew what to do with that. As her slim fingers reached the sensitive regions, Glenn felt as if he might explode—not in the sexual sense, but sheerly from sensory overload and excitement. One could only say that Sasha looked like sex, moved like sex... when he kissed her, she tasted like sex, and anytime she touched him, anywhere, it simply was... sex.

Then her hand moved away, replaced by soft, warm, wet lips, and a pleasing warmth spread throughout his body. Her head bobbed smoothly up and down, a practiced expert. She had found his gearshift and was working him like a professional driver on a closed course.

Through all the frantic sensory reports rose a rational thought in Glenn's mind—an uncomfortable, unwelcome thought, like a corpse rising to the surface of a lake: *You shouldn't be doing this*. He considered it for a moment, then pushed it back down, preferring to focus on those warm lips and that persistent tongue...

Sasha came up for air, gasping, and let out a powerful moan, as if pleasuring him had also pleasured her. Maybe it had. "You like?" she breathed with a smile.

"Mmm."

"I'm doing good?"

"Mmm-hmm."

"Mmm." She laughed softly, delighting in his wordless response. Suddenly, she launched into an exaggerated southern accent. "I can even sound like her if you wannnnt."

Glenn's eyes were aimed at the ceiling, but instead he saw Ashley, laying on the elevator floor, looking somehow deflated. He felt his body cool immediately. He could not control it, but even if he could, he wouldn't have stopped it. Sasha sounded like a Milwaukee-born starlet auditioning for *The Dukes of Hazzard*. Ashley did not sound like that at all. *Had* not sounded like that. Her Alabama lilt was soft and endearing... hearing it lifted his spirits without fail. And he would never hear it again. He thought of the snow angel...

Sasha moved to continue her work, even though the situation down there was rapidly becoming moot. "Stop it," he said.

"Sure thing," she said, not stopping.

Glenn sat up, grasped her shoulders and pushed her away. Sasha simply smiled and bounced back onto him. "That can be a fun game too."

He pushed her back again and tucked everything away—not as quick and simple as it sounds. She was on him again quickly, kissing his face. He pushed her again, touching something soft in the process. Was that...? Yeah. She stumbled backward and bumped against the desk.

"I'm not doing this," he said. "Not..." He looked at her. She looked as if she had bitten into a lemon. "Not... not now," he finished, standing. He took a few steps toward the door and his shirt. "Later, maybe."

"Later is not happening," she said through tight lips. He looked back; she was crouched, back against the desk, a childlike look of defiance on her face. "Right now, or not at all."

An uncomfortable heat began to burn in his chest. For a few moments, his eyes remained glued to her—topless, her lanky frame curled up almost defensively. Then he picked up his shirt.

"I gotta do my laundry."

3

Glenn limped up the stairs toward his floor. A tense soreness had developed in his crotch... right below where Sasha had been working. *Too bad no one's getting married; I could provide something blue.* Thoughts were flooding back into his mind—rational, sensible thoughts—a function of his brain that had been greatly reduced when Sasha kissed him, and basically shut down once her hand had gone south. He could almost feel the lights turning back on in the factory of his mind.

He had felt this soreness before. The last time, because a girl named Ann had refused to go any further on the first date. And before that, because his parents had come home unexpectedly early, interrupting a session of timid exploration with a girl from high school named Crystal. Never before had he ended it voluntarily and, in essence, brought this feeling upon himself.

Glenn's head seemed to be radiating heat. How... what... why...? He stopped on the third floor landing and leaned against the wall. She had lured him there... for sex. Yes, she had. THE Sasha W. Goldsmith: adored by some, tolerated by many, hated by the rest... but KNOWN by all. The epitome of sex for every male student on campus. The flirt... the bitch... the legend. But... why him? An inarticulate feeling of isolation swept through him. The few people he trusted enough to tell about this were gone for Thanksgiving. The dorm was practically empty.

Empty...

And that was it. He and Eric might have been the only guys in the building right now. Sasha had limited options. His spirits sagged further. He had been chosen by default.

He whirled and swung his fist, pounding it against the textured wall. It hurt. "Stupid..." he said aimlessly. "Why don't you fuck your boyfriend?!" He felt horny, angry, and guilty. Sasha had made him feel this way. And, at the moment, he hated her for it. Something else accompanied that hatred, like a stowaway... a searing bitterness toward himself for leaving. It coiled and slithered through his mind like a snake, rattling its tail defensively any time his thoughts approached it. This was the part of himself that would have enjoyed—rapturously—wrapping himself around that tall, skinny girl, putting skin against skin, and making that waterbed churn. Yes, she had been with a lot of guys—that was the point! She knew exactly what to do, from experience... exactly where to touch them and how and exactly what positions to assume to assure maximum pleasure. This was why so many guys had tolerated her unpredictable behavior for any length of time. Sasha seemed to lack inhibitions. He had seen her several times, checking her mailbox in nothing but a towel, or a bra and panties. During these excursions, she would smile and speak to every marginally attractive guy who passed by, but ignore any fellow girls. *This woman would suck you dry and wait patiently until you could go again. You know it. And you screwed it up, on purpose.*

He couldn't argue with this angry part of himself, not

while his balls were throbbing and he could recall the taste of her mouth. There is a certain kind of madness that affects a man when he is sexually aroused. He may think and do things that later seem stupid... but everything changes once he is satisfied. Glenn, of course, was not satisfied, so the madness was still upon him. He knew this at some level and accepted it. Confronting those feelings, while they were fresh, might send him straight back to Sasha's room. The larger, more rational part of him was in control now... if only barely.

He rested his forehead against the cool drywall and leaned there for a minute. The soreness persisted. Best to just get on with life, he decided, and hopefully something would take his mind off the pain.

Eric looked much too comfortable on the couch, one leg curled underneath him, staring at his laptop. Sitting next to the computer was an open beer bottle. Glenn stared at it for a moment, then shuffled over to the kitchen, trying hard not to disturb his aching crotch.

Eric finally looked at him. "Dude... did you pull something?"

Glenn, holding back a grimace, didn't return the look. Yes, something had been pulled. By Eric's girlfriend. Glenn was staring at the blank white face of the refrigerator, but he was seeing the top of Sasha's head, bobbing up and down energetically, her hair flying wildly. What to say? Tell him that his girlfriend was cheating? That line of thought had undeniable appeal... a rare opportunity to cut down Eric's ever-present swagger. An opportunity that had, well, almost literally fallen into his lap. He could use it now. He could hurt Eric immediately. But... there seemed to be something deeper here. Sasha wasn't just cheating in the typical, bored-with-her-boyfriend sense... it seemed as if she couldn't help herself. She had been on her way to his suite, scantily clad and overly flirty, in the traditional Sasha fashion. And she had wanted it NOW. Despite the fact that she had never pursued him before. Glenn shivered slightly as the final tumbler clicked into place, unlocking a previously hidden realization: she would do it again. And again. It was as if she needed it. After the holiday break, the dorm would be populated again and she could pick from dozens of guys who would never dream of telling her no.

Glenn looked at Eric from the corner of his eye. Telling him about this now would be... almost merciful. It would allow him to get out before he got too attached, sparing him unnecessary heartache. A good friend would open up and tell Eric the truth—that his girlfriend was untrustworthy and unfaithful. Glenn was not his friend. Glenn would allow Eric to remain blissfully ignorant as his girlfriend dragged men she hardly knew into her pink room. He would find out eventually... and he would wish he had known sooner.

Eric took a swig of beer and brought down his bottle hard enough onto the table to grab Glenn's attention. "I think something did get pulled," said Glenn.

"Exercise more," said Eric. "Take the stairs instead of the elevator."

"Good advice," Glenn replied, opening the refrigerator. Seeing Eric's beer had made him wonder. He hadn't bought any beer recently... but maybe Craig had. Alas, the only beverage in the fridge was water. Glenn stared at it ruefully, then took a bottle. He had worked up a hint of perspiration in Sasha's room, and sadly, his soda was irretrievable.

Glenn sauntered into the living area. Every light in the suite was turned on because, well, the electricity was included in the rent. Eric had settled into the couch, his laptop sitting just close enough so he could click through a web page, looking detached. Glenn approached the two large front windows, where bluish light filtered through.

White Friday

He pushed aside the blinds and looked outside: a thick carpet of white covered everything. Waves of thick snowflakes still filled the air. He could see no tire tracks anywhere, and no evidence of any life in the area. The sun had barely showed up for work today, and now it seemed to be clock-watching, waiting for the moment it could punch out and head home for the weekend.

"We're trapped here," Glenn said. It wasn't a completely bad feeling; he welcomed the occasional isolation. The quiet. The freedom. He might have felt completely comfortable in this situation, even with Eric hanging around. The pall of Ashley's fate, however, had darkened everything. And rightfully so. She had been special... not just pleasantly different, but special to him. If this weekend was to be spent in quiet, isolated mourning, then... so be it.

"It's not that bad," said Eric.

Glenn touched the window, something his parents had vehemently taught him not to do. A chill spread through his body. It reminded him of Sasha's cold hands... though the rest of her had been noticeably warmer. "It's peachy for you," he said, with just a pinch of sarcasm. "You've got your cold beer and your hot girlfriend..."

"She's not just hot. She's very... passionate. She really cares."

"It's great to be you, isn't it?" The words came out with a thinner shell of sarcasm than he had intended.

Out of the corner of his eye, he saw Eric sit up. "You sound tense. Maybe if you got laid..."

Glenn sighed. Of course that would be Eric's answer. He seemed to have a renewed interest in his laptop. "You and Ashley could do each other some good," he was saying.

Glenn sniffed defiantly. "Indeed..."

Eric stared at his computer screen for a few moments. "Her away message says she's doing laundry. Aren't you doing laundry?"

"Last time I checked," said Glenn. It seemed like days had passed since he'd loaded those washing machines.

"So, why don't you go and *check* on it?"

Glenn was staring at the window, but he wasn't seeing the window. "Is Sasha online?"

Eric paused. "No. But she's not speaking to me, anyway."

Glenn turned toward him, intrigued. "Oh? What did you do?"

"We had a disagreement."

"An argument, you mean."

"No," Eric sighed. "A disagreement, that's all it takes. But she'll want me back in a day or two."

Glenn thought about the emptiness of the dorm. "Maybe sooner."

Eric smiled. "Optimism, I like it. Now what about you and Ash?"

Glenn shook his head, a little too quickly.

"Come on. I think she likes you. I'm rarely wrong about these things."

Glenn paced nervously. "Laundry is... a personal thing. I don't want to walk in on her while she's... folding her underwear or something." He ended up sitting on the arm of a chair, his eyes fixed on the carpet.

Eric stared at him for a moment, then smirked and stood up. He approached Glenn and stood over him, looking confident. "Let me tell you a secret."

Glenn looked up at him. "Okay..." He could faintly smell beer, and some kind of earthy aroma.

"Girls are human. Just like us. They eat, sleep, burp, fart, piss, shit... and a few other things that even we don't do."

"I know," said Glenn.

"So, quit treating them like... some kind of magical creatures that are above you! Quit worshiping them!"

"I wouldn't say that I—"

"If you don't go down there, I will. And I'll tell her you like her."

Glenn's annoyance was growing. "Okay. Go ahead."

Eric scoffed and stepped into the dining area. "Pussy. You have been with a girl before, right?"

Glenn thought for a moment. "More than you realize."

"I'll bet they initiated the contact."

"You are so *smart*!" exclaimed Glenn, in such a blatant imitation of Sasha that he almost made himself laugh.

"A sarcastic pussy," said Eric as he opened the front door. "Wonderful."

"Aren't those the best kind?" Glenn called after him. The door swung shut; Eric had gone.

Glenn sat there for a minute, hunched over, glaring angrily at the floor. Then he stormed over to the door and turned the lock.

His phone erupted with "Mary Jane's Last Dance"—his default ring tone. He didn't recognize the number, but it was local, so he answered it anyway.

A stern voice spoke to him: "Is this Glenn? At the dorm at Tomlin University?"

"Yeah."

"Hello, Glenn. My name is Wayne. I'm an Emergency Medical Technician, we got the call about your situation, and we'll be there as soon as we can. The problem is, there don't seem to be many roads cleared out in your area, so we have to hook up with a city plow or we won't get very far."

"Okay."

"Just make sure the body is safe and no one moves it. Now, if we get another call where someone's life is in danger, we'll have to take care of that first. Otherwise... conservative estimate... we should be there within an hour. Okay?"

"Y-yeah," said Glenn, suddenly a little anxious. That

was very okay, compared with the previous two-hour estimate.

Sliding the phone back in his pocket, he thought of Ashley's body, curled up and deflated under the laundry room table. His annoyance had dissipated... what if Eric nosed around in there?

Damn.

Glenn shot out of his suite, running faster than he had in years.

Running, running, running.

As a running back in high school, he hadn't been the fast guy. No, Glenn was the guy who came in when the fast guy, the starter, needed to catch his breath. Only once or twice, in two seasons, had Glenn ever outrun anyone. His talent was breaking tackles, keeping his legs moving, refusing to go down until three or four or five opponents had piled onto him.

He paused to catch his breath in the first floor hallway before it turned toward the laundry room. Upon turning the corner, he saw Eric standing at the door, staring in through the window. Eric turned toward him, gave a sympathetic smile and said, "She's not here."

What? Glenn felt every organ in his torso seize up. She had to be here, she couldn't—

Wait. Glenn forced a breath in and out. Right. As far as Eric knew, she wasn't there. And... in reality... she really wasn't.

Eric stared at him for a moment, perhaps mistaking his expression for one of disappointment. "Come to apologize?"

Glenn brushed past him, pushing the door open. "I came to check my laundry." The curled up form of Ashley looked undisturbed beneath the table. Glenn stepped slowly over to the machine washing his colors... it had finished already. Probably five or ten minutes ago, in fact; he had lost track of time somewhere between Eric and Sasha. Now the wet clothes were just stewing in there. He didn't have quarters on him for the dryer, or cash for the change machine; he'd have to go back upstairs. Dumbass... he should have thought before dashing down here. Laundry: the bane of a student's existence. He kicked the empty water bottle that still lay on the floor. Eons ago, it seemed, he had set off to get some extra laundry money after exchanging five quarters for a bottle of soda.

A sound came from his pocket, a text message. He took out his phone and looked at the name on the screen: Ashley Freeman.

He stared at the screen for almost a minute, trying to see past the pixels. It was getting warm in here. He glanced toward the window in the door: no Eric. Then he knelt by the table, lifted the corner of his comforter, and there she was, curled up, motionless: Ashley Freeman. Her hair obscured her face... maybe that was for the best.

His thumb twitched toward the phone screen and touched it furtively, opening the text message: **I'm bored. Wanna come over?**

Glenn exhaled, feeling as if he had shed a sauna suit and stepped into an actual sauna. An uncomfortable warmth remained, but it seemed less personal: he was not going crazy, nor was he being pursued by Ashley's ghost. But someone was trying to play him, for certain. Ashley had never used lazy contractions like 'wanna' or 'gonna' in any written communication.

Someone had her phone.

The uncomfortable warmth seemed to intensify; someone was in that sauna with him, but a deceitful steam kept him from seeing who it was. His phone hand trembled with a nervous uncertainty. He slowly typed a response to the text message: **Ssure, I'll be there sooon.**

After correcting his shaky spelling, he pressed the send button. The message took flight. It wouldn't have to travel far, nor contend with the snow.

4

Glenn left the laundry room, having adjusted the comforter so that Ashley's form looked as innocuous as possible. Now, he had no choice but to visit Ashley's room... right? Whoever had her phone must have known about her... condition. They were posing as her, after all. Perhaps whoever it was wanted to hurt him as well. Why else would they lure him to Ashley's suite?

Yes, he was being lured. And he didn't like it. But... he had to find out who had Ashley's phone. There was no other way... right?

He stopped in the hall and typed a quick text to Ashley's phone: **Why don't you come over here?** He hesitated for a moment, then sent it. He sighed and stared down the long, bland hallway. This was all just too crazy. And at the moment, there was no one in the building he could trust. He typed another text: **Wish you were here, man**. That one went to Craig.

The halls were empty and completely silent, but the fluorescent lights above still glowed, as they did twenty-four hours a day. Glenn trudged up the stairs, facing the snowy expanse through the windows at each landing. The campus looked like a great white sheet of paper, or the empty screen of a word processing program... either way, something a student like him would eventually need to fill.

At the third floor landing, his phone chimed. A response from "Ashley": **My bed is better than urs ;)**

Glenn stared at it in disbelief. Obviously, Ashley wouldn't use "urs." But the innuendo spread through his head like octopus ink, clouding his thoughts... his rational thoughts, anyway. He stood there for about a minute, the response running through his head.

When his mind regained its traction, his first thought was this: who knows that Ashley likes me? Yes, she had liked him; he knew it when he saw her writings online, but it had taken him a while to acknowledge it. Mostly because he hadn't dated anyone since his sophomore year of college, and he had actually become comfortable with his singleness. It was like getting into a swimming pool: unpleasantly chilly at first, but it became more and more tolerable as time went on. He didn't *want* to be in that particular pool, but the water was nice enough, and as long as he was in there, he might as well enjoy it. And he had eventually reasoned that college life was complicated enough without a relationship to keep up. The other thing that had given him pause was this: unlike the previous girls Glenn had pursued, Ashley could not have been described as "hot." She was not tall or in particularly good shape; she didn't have large breasts, long legs or a firm ass; she didn't dress provocatively or party and she wasn't overly flirty. He'd liked the intangible things about her. The things that couldn't be seen. And this was new. This was... mature. So, what if her feelings had been equally deep? That could have led to something... big.

The person using Ashley's phone knew about their

mutual attraction; they were using it to lure him in. And not in the most subtle way, either.

Glenn stepped slowly out of the stairwell and trudged down the hall. He stopped at his door and listened for a few moments. No sounds.

Ashley's suite was down the hall, where the corner turned outward. He walked toward it slowly, feeling numb. He had taken this route several times in the past, hoping to see her... and once or twice, it had worked. More often, however, all he saw were the quaint seasonal decorations on her door. Far more often he saw her roommate, Sam, an athletic, outgoing girl who looked as though she had a little Native American blood in her. Sam apparently took part in as many sports and student organizations as her free time would allow; she was always on her way somewhere, meeting with some team or group. She seemed to know almost everyone in the building. She exercised frequently and strictly controlled her diet. And, for a few months earlier in the fall, she had spent much of her down time with Eric. It was a match-up that Glenn couldn't quite understand, but that wasn't unusual. As long as people were free to date whomever they wanted, odd and unexpected couplings would happen. Sam was attractive, smart, fun and dedicated. Glenn wouldn't have said no if she had asked *him* out... but he wouldn't have adjusted his route to chance an encounter with her, either. Maybe she was too perfect... he hadn't really thought about it. There was no doubt in his mind, however, that she was too good for Eric, who had probably just been interested in her body. They'd had fun together, sure, but to Glenn it just seemed that Sam was getting a raw deal. Perhaps she had realized that when she finally dumped him.

Another chime from his phone; another text. Glenn looked at his phone—this one came from Craig. Yeah, like he could really help from... wherever he had gone. For a moment, Glenn idly wondered if Craig had left his R.A. keys in the suite somewhere. As a Resident Assistant, Craig carried around a set of keys that would open any door in the building. Those could be useful, even if just to keep Ashley's body safely in the first floor office. Or perhaps Craig surrendered the keys when his shifts ended... Glenn didn't know. He opened the text message... it said: **405**.

Glenn stared at it for a few seconds, then shook his head. "Crazy." He looked up—Ashley's suite. He had to. No more procrastinating.

He walked up to the door and faced it. The eyes on the scarecrows were dead center, staring him down. One of them appeared to be female—eyelashes, longer straw "hair"... they were happy together. But... wouldn't a decoration depicting a couple indicate... an actual couple? Glenn pondered this for a moment, moving his gaze toward the number on the door: 309.

Hmm. 309... 405?

Holy crap. It was a room number.

Glenn was not accustomed to the flat auburn shade of the carpet on the fourth floor. The ceilings were slightly lower up here, and slanted inward in some corners, giving it kind of a cramped attic feel. The doors were closer together... all single apartments. Apartment 405 was right above his own bedroom.

He knocked... a bit more timidly than he had intended. What if he had jumped to the wrong conclusion, and "405" meant something else entirely? That would be... awkward. Was that movement he heard behind the door? Someone looking through the peephole, maybe? He remembered that this was Chuck's apartment just as the doorknob began to turn.

The door swung inward quickly. The dim lighting

inside revealed very little. Whoever had opened the door was standing back, concealed in shadow. Glenn hesitated, staring. A hushed, yet slightly mocking voice came forth: "Don't be afraid." Glenn recognized it. He stepped forward into the darkness. The door swung shut behind him.

Ensconced in darkness, he realized that there was a single source of light in the apartment: a TV against a far wall, showing a muted John Wayne movie. The TV light illuminated the standard dorm furniture, but not much more, and there was no sound. The entire room seemed to be muted.

It must have been ten seconds before the familiar voice spoke, at a normal volume this time: "Eyes adjust to the dark yet?"

"Yeah," said Glenn, starting to relax.

A tsunami of light flooded the room. Glenn let out a sharp moan and snapped his eyes shut, however too late. It wasn't exactly painful, but damn close.

Craig let out a single goofy chuckle, his signature laugh, from his position next to the light switches.

Glenn turned toward the sound, though he couldn't quite open his eyes yet. "A normal person would apologize."

"Only the weak apologize!" came the response. There was a smile evident in his voice. "You used my clippers!"

"Yeah, well, you said I could..."

"Looks good."

Glenn slowly opened his eyes, blinking rapidly. After a few seconds, he could make out the image of his roommate standing near the door, wearing nothing but his form-fitting boxer briefs. This was not uncommon—Craig preferred to relax this way. At least he was in decent shape; Glenn was one hundred percent straight, but if he had to see a scantily-clad male body, he'd prefer it be a fit one. Needless to say, the girls admired Craig's body as well. He had strong, yet slightly juvenile-looking facial features that seemed to say, "You can rely on me... but don't turn your back on me!" His stature and body shape were very similar to Glenn—they could have borrowed each other's clothing if they had been into that kind of thing. The identical buzzed haircuts made them look even more alike. As silhouettes, they would be just about indistinguishable.

Glenn looked around the single apartment; it actually seemed well-kept. The counters and table looked spotless, utensils all had their places, DVDs all lined up neatly on the shelf under the TV...

"This is Chuck's place, isn't it?"

Craig nodded. "Mm-hmm."

Glenn felt a vague pang of guilt swim through his system. Aside from an elaborate samurai figure in the kitchen and a poster for something called "Death Note" on the living room wall, it did not match his expectations for the dwelling of a sloppy-looking overweight anime fan.

"He let me stay here for the weekend," said Craig.

Glenn affixed him with a firm gaze. "Why?"

Craig thought for a moment. "Because we're friends," he said, as if that answered the question.

"I mean... why stay here? What's wrong with... our place?" A small sprout of a thought had surfaced—that perhaps Craig had wanted to get away from him.

"Oh," said Craig, considering. "I wanted to... get away. That's what holidays are for, right? I don't have anywhere else to go."

Glenn nodded, feeling a bit awkward.

"I figured it would be kind of like a vacation if no one knew I was here. No one to answer to but myself. I am on duty, though." He pointed to a pager and a set of about twenty keys lying on the living room table.

"Any pages so far?"

White Friday

Craig shook his head. "Nope. It's just been me... myself... and the John Wayne marathon."

Glenn sat down on the arm of a living room chair, trying to process all of this. "Ignorance is bliss, huh?"

Craig took a few steps toward him. "Yeah, and let's keep it that way."

Glenn looked up, uncertain. Huh?

"The game last night. Don't spoil it for me, I haven't seen it yet."

"Who has?" Glenn wished a game was his biggest problem. "It was on the football network, remember?"

"Oh yeah," said Craig, softening.

"I'd be surprised if anyone here saw it," Glenn murmured.

Craig looked at the carpet for a moment. "Sasha."

Glenn looked up again. "Huh?"

"Sasha has all those extra channels."

"You would know, wouldn't you?"

"Yeah." Craig's lips split into a knowing grin. "Yeah, I would."

Glenn stared at the space between Craig's feet. *Should I tell him?* What would he think? A guy, letting himself be dragged into a girl's room and... and what? Seduced? Yeah, that's what he would call it. But what would be worse... letting himself be seduced, or... refusing to go through with it? One way or another, he would not come out looking good. Part of him knew that these thoughts were crazy, but... this was college. And a guy was expected to behave in certain ways around girls. If you can get sex from any moderately attractive girl, you're expected to do it. If you don't, you're a coward or a prude, or... just someone who doesn't like sex. Any college guy who doesn't like sex is considered an oddity, maybe even a freak. Still... he had to tell someone about... everything. He had just found out that his most trusted friend was here, now, in the building. There was really no question of what to do.

"Well, you're not the only one in this room..." Glenn said shakily.

Craig crossed his arms and adopted a no-bullshit stance. "What's this?"

"I was... a guest of Sasha, earlier today." How might Craig respond... disbelief? Jealousy? Anger?

Craig smiled. "You entered her pink room, huh?"

Glenn, having no idea how to respond, simply smiled back.

Craig was nodding in encouragement. "How was it?"

Glenn tried to think about it, but all he could do was sigh and shake his head. "I don't know how I feel, it's just... I have to get my thoughts sorted out..."

"It's okay, man, you're not the first to fall victim to a Sasha sneak attack."

Glenn stared blankly at his roommate.

"She's like Jaws, man. Without the teeth."

"Thank God for that," Glenn mumbled. But there were stranger things happening than Sasha's advances. He looked up at Craig. "Can I show you something?"

Craig laughed. "Dude, you're better off showing it to a doctor."

Five minutes later, Glenn stepped quietly out of the west-end stairwell into the first floor hall. Craig followed, having put on a pair of socks and a slim-fit t-shirt. They approached the laundry room slowly—Glenn constantly watching for others, Craig watching his roommate with thinly veiled amusement. When they reached the laundry room and looked inside, there was indeed a shape under the comforter. A strange thought had occurred to Glenn, that perhaps this had all been a delusion of his, a product of his overactive imagination, even a dream mistaken for reality. Perhaps if he saw it through Craig's eyes, this nightmare would dissipate and... reality would ensue. But the comforter was still under the table, and there was still a human-sized shape under it.

Glenn looked nervously at Craig and stepped inside. Craig followed, saying nothing. Glenn knelt beside the table, touched the comforter gently, and gestured for Craig to come near. Once the gray-socked feet entered his peripheral vision, he braced for his roommate's reaction and lifted the comforter, revealing...

...an overturned laundry basket. The same one that had been there when he'd come down to load his clothes. It was the same basic size and shape as a petite young woman in a fetal position. The young woman, however... Ashley... was not there.

Craig exhaled loudly. "I knew it."

Glenn was looking around frantically. No other place in the room to hide a body. "What?"

"I knew you'd try to trick me somehow. I came down here because I felt bad, about not telling you I was staying here. Well, you got me for once." He was moving toward the door.

"But—no," sputtered Glenn. "She was—here. Someone... fucking... took her!"

Craig stopped. Looked back over his shoulder. Glenn didn't usually swear. Not like that. "Okay... I deceived you... you tricked me... it's all good. Come on, *The Searchers* is on."

Glenn stood, grabbed the basket and advanced on Craig. "This is... NOT a trick," he growled, flinging the basket at his roommate's feet. Craig, startled, reached out to push him away, but Glenn seized a fistful of Craig's shirt, holding him in place. "This is real."

Craig stared at him with a calm-before-the-storm expression. "You sure?"

The storm might have come if not for a chime from Glenn's phone. He pulled away and read his newly-received text message. Then he looked up to meet Craig's icy gaze. "If you care at all about Ashley, you'll help me find her."

Craig's expression opened up with this, the first mention of Ashley's name.

"I've never seen you like that. It is okay to be assertive, you know. You just might get what you want."

Glenn just stared at him, trying to keep his somber expression in place. Cracking a smile would only betray the sinking feeling in his gut, as well as the cold vacancy in his chest. And yet... Craig had diffused the tense situation, just like that. And he had done it by speaking the truth.

"Okay. Where's Ashley?"

Glenn exhaled slowly and closed his eyes. "I..." He paused for a moment to think. "I'm not sure... I think something might be wrong." Craig would just think he was crazy if he told the truth. It was the truth... wasn't it? He had held Ashley's lifeless body in his arms, he had carried her here and covered her with his comforter... He hadn't dreamed it. He couldn't have. It was real. It WAS real.

Craig saw the confusion on Glenn's face. "You need help?"

Glenn just nodded.

5

Craig knocked on the door to Ashley and Sam's suite. He hadn't bothered to put on pants; Ashley wouldn't mind. She'd just laugh and move on. She was cute, for sure... sometimes even ridiculously cute, but he had never been interested in her. Well... once. But he had quickly realized that she wasn't his type. They had a good friendship, though... not necessarily deep, but solid enough. That was probably why Glenn had asked him to check on her.

He had agreed because Glenn had been upset enough to use the f-word. For Glenn, that signaled near-nuclear levels of emotion. Sure, he occasionally would use *damn* or *what the hell*, but his *son-of-a*'s always trailed off into nothing, and *fucks* were few and far between. Craig had no such qualms. They were just words, right? Besides, sometimes *fuck* was called for. There was some movie character he had admired who preferred *fucking* over *making love*. Sure, it was vulgar in people's minds. But sometimes you had to be vulgar to express the intensity of your feelings. Love and romance have their place, but everyone appreciates a good fuck now and then!

He heard a female voice, faintly, through the door. He knocked again, harder. The voice came again, slightly shrill this time, but he could make out the words: "Come iiiiin!" There was a definite southern twang; sometimes her accent came through more strongly when she was upset.

The door was unlocked. The suite was… entirely dark. Lights off, blinds closed, curtains (where there were curtains) closed. Craig let go of the door and watched the rectangle of light from the hall slowly disappear.

The voice came from his left: "I'm in my bedroom, Glenn." *Glay-yen.* Shrill and overly twangy. Not Ashley. This sounded more like a pathetic attempt at imitating a southern accent.

Craig had deliberately remained silent. The darkness told him that something was off. Now he knew that the girl in Ashley's bedroom thought he was Glenn, and as long as he didn't identify himself, he had an advantage. Unless she turned on the lights, she wouldn't realize her mistake. And frankly, this situation… the uncertainty and the calculated deception of it all… kind of turned him on.

His eyes adjusted; there was just enough light to make out walls and doorways. But then, all the suites had the same layout anyway. He stepped carefully toward the bedroom, hands held out to find the edges of the doorway.

"You know me," came the voice, still twangy, but with a touch of sweetness. "I finished all my homework two days ago. I've been here all alone with nothing to do. Are you coming in?" *Ee-in?*

Craig stepped through the doorway. She was there, on the left, where the bed was typically situated. He could hear her small movements; she must have been laying on it. Straight ahead, where the window would be, was nothing. No light seeping through at all… she must have covered it with more than just the standard blinds. The room was completely dark.

"I feel so isolated with the snow and my roomie gone," she cooed. "I know she's not far away, but that don't really help."

Craig looked to his left but... there was nothing to see.

"I asked you here because... well... I've never been with a guy. I think maybe now might be the right time."

Craig smiled. Would Glenn have fallen for this? Probably... but it wasn't necessary. For the real Ashley, Glenn would have needed zero enticement. And Glenn was no prude. He was just... conservative... when it came to relationships. He preferred to keep life simple, and only go after girls he knew would match well with him, rather than any girl who turned him on. At least that's how it seemed to Craig.

"Don't be nervous, Glenn. I'm not. The snow makes it kind of romantic, don't ya think?"

If it's so romantic, let's open the window and see it! She did have a sexy voice, though. He thought he could almost recognize it, beneath the affected accent. The sounds of her moving, the breathiness of her voice, it was all getting to him. He moved closer to the bed.

A smooth female hand reached out and found his. "I know we're both kind of shy... but I've had a crush on you for a while." She stroked his hand.

Craig was getting excited, no way around it. This girl had clearly set out to seduce someone... and it was working.

He heard her shifting on the bed and her other hand came into contact with his jockey shorts. "Hey there." She smoothly undid the button. "Don't worry, Glenn. I know what to do..."

Once Craig had started moving, there was no stopping him. Lips met lips, skin met skin, and the next thing he knew, he was in her. His arms encircled a long, slender torso. The southern accent melted away as she moaned.

And at some point, Craig realized he was fucking Sasha.

Glenn stepped into his suite. Eric was there. He had tuned the TV to the John Wayne marathon. He was also laying across the couch, shirtless.

"Dude," said Eric in greeting.

"Comfortable?"

"This couch? Oh, man... this couch... I love it..." Eric looked sleepy, yet somehow still energized.

Glenn stepped closer. "Don't you have the same one?"

"I guess I do, but, man... I love this."

Glenn moved toward the kitchen. "Just don't make love to it."

Eric let out a half-hearted chuckle and turned up the TV volume.

Glenn opened the refrigerator. He knew he'd finished the last of the juice yesterday, but... hell, maybe that had been just a dream, too. He wasn't sure what to expect anymore. Perhaps if he looked outside, he'd find a sunny spring day.

The only liquid in the fridge was water. Still. This was probably a good thing; no sugary soft drinks or dehydrating alcohol. He and Craig were pretty good about eating and drinking healthy... Craig especially. Still, a nice cold beer to mellow him out would have been just fine.

His bottle of water was in the living room where he'd left it. He took it to the dining area—a round table between the entrance and the kitchen—and sat down. The table was clean for once, bare aside from its one decoration: a bulbous glass vase filled with water and... a betta fish.

Glenn slumped in the sparse wooden chair and stared at the little red and blue creature as it drifted lazily...

White Friday

August 22nd... a Saturday.

A day of pervasive heat, so very common in the latter half of the summer. On those days, the very act of wearing clothes becomes an inconvenience, and the possibility of a sudden, refreshing rain becomes a desirable fantasy.

Glenn was sweating more than he normally would have; moving into a new room will do that, even one with central air. He had graduated... from undergrad to graduate student, and, coincidentally, from the first floor to the third floor.

He set down the last box in his new bedroom, pushed sweaty hair off his forehead and looked around. What he saw was a blank, vacant, meaningless space. But it was now his dwelling space, and soon it would become a reflection of him, and a vital part of his life. However, something else had stuck in his mind, from his small talk with his new roommate a few minutes ago.

He stepped out into the common area. Craig was leaning against a kitchen counter, looking bored and somehow expectant.

"You mentioned football."

"I said no such thing, and you can't prove I did!"

Glenn's mouth hung open for a few seconds. "You just said it like two minutes ago."

"*Touché*," said Craig, smiling.

"Did you mean like, tackle football?"

"If there is another kind, I don't want to know about it."

"Can anyone play?"

Craig looked a little wary. "Anyone?"

"Where can I sign up?"

Craig exhaled and inhaled before answering. "You wanna go get something to eat? There's a waffle house down the street."

"Come on. I can play!"

Craig gave him an appraising look—though not entirely judgmental. "You're just too... eh."

Glenn understood; he had heard it before. Too passive, too withdrawn... football players were thought to be all macho and extroverted, although no one would come out and say it. But he had played just fine in high school and he just wanted that feeling again. The feeling of knocking guys around on the field, asserting his will and... winning. The competitive fire didn't always show on the outside... but it was there. Tomlin U had a division I football team, yes—the Mercenaries—but they were usually terrible. Besides, conditioning, practicing and playing for the "real" team would take up more time than he was willing to spend. There was an intramural league, though, as Craig had just mentioned... "I played in high school. I was a running back!"

"Right," said Craig.

Glenn sighed. "You don't care, do you?"

Craig stared into space for a few seconds, then shrugged. "We have enough guys."

Glenn stared at the floor. His exhaustion was starting to catch up to him. The plain wooden chairs in the dining area were starting to look good; next thing he knew, he had slumped down into one of them. He leaned in toward the vase in the center of the table. The little fish swam forward to give him a look.

"That's little Craig. He's about a year old."

"Like, Craig Junior?" Glenn asked lazily.

"No... Craig Junior is in my pants. And he's not little."

"Oh." Yeah. If that kind of bravado was necessary to make the football team, Glenn felt content being excluded.

"Hungry?" Craig asked.

"Yeah." Despite the awkward start, Glenn wanted to forge a good relationship with his roommate.

White Friday

"Waffle House?"

"Uhh..." He needed to be careful with money, considering he was living on student loans and twenty hours a week of minimum wage. But this seemed like a good occasion to eat out. And, he reminded himself, his summer income allowed him to splurge a little bit more. "We can do better than that, can't we?"

"Okay," said Craig, sounding pleasantly surprised, as he moved toward his bedroom. "Let me get my keys."

Glenn sat back and relaxed for a moment. Then came a knock at the door—firm enough to be heard, but not loud.

Glenn sat there for a moment, watching for Craig to return. Then he remembered: this was his place now, too. He jumped up as a voice carried through the door, a smooth female voice with a hint of a southern drawl: "Hellooo?"

He opened the door. There stood a girl, at least six inches shorter than him, with tanned skin, dark blond hair pulled back into a single braid... a pleasant grin on her face. And her eyes, alight with genuine enthusiasm. "Hi," she said. "Are you Craig's new roommate?"

"Well, yes," Glenn said, trying to think. It was proving difficult at the moment. "I'm not technically new, though. I lived downstairs last year."

"I see," she said. "Well, I'm Ashley." She shifted what she was holding—which, Glenn realized, was a large bowl full of snicker doodles—and shook his hand.

"Glenn," he said, and when she smiled up at him, he forgot where he was.

"You gonna let her in?" came a voice from behind him. Craig's voice. Glenn jerked his head around to see his new roommate, looking amused. "It's okay, she's not dangerous."

"Not that you know of," Ashley replied.

Glenn stepped back and held the door open. "Come in,

please."

She stepped inside. "I made these for my cool neighbors, but... they're not around. So I thought you guys might like them instead."

"I could pretend to be offended," said Craig, "but it'd just be pretend... hell, I don't mind sloppy seconds!"

"Eww," Ashley said, setting the bowl on the table. "I don't want to know." Craig sat down and bit into a cookie, immediately making "mmm" sounds. Ashley watched, smiling, then turned to Glenn. "How come I haven't seen you around?"

Glenn hesitated, looking for the answer he already knew. "I was home all summer. Working... making sandwiches... yeah..." He trailed off awkwardly as Ashley nodded, looking interested. "You... when did you move in?"

"June. Not in time for the first summer session, but the second... I wanted to get settled in here..."

Glenn realized that Craig was watching him, grinning. Craig spoke up: "Glenn was just telling me about his high school football career."

Ashley's eyes lit up. "Yeah?"

"Yeah," said Glenn. "I was a... running back. I had, um... 538 yards, 6 touchdowns my senior year... as a backup." He had learned to qualify his statistics with that last phrase, otherwise they would seem rather mundane.

"Nice!" said Craig, actually sounding impressed.

Glenn began to feel warm, between Ashley's interest and Craig's reaction. "Yeah... they called me Bruce Banner."

Craig erupted in laughter, and then coughing. Cookie crumbs flew from his mouth.

Ashley gave him a stern look, clearly not concerned. "What?"

Craig sputtered: "That's the name of the Hulk, when he's not the Hulk!"

White Friday

Glenn just stared at his roommate. It was nothing new to him. It may have been a sarcastic nickname, but it had come with respect nonetheless. He was a steady guy, they had all said, but he had the power inside of him.

As Craig giggled to himself, Ashley turned and shared with Glenn a look of pure empathy. "Well, if you guys like football," she said, "perhaps we can watch some together. If you like Alabama, that is."

"Boooo!" called Craig through cupped hands. "Go Tar Heels!" Ashley gave him a mock-angry look.

"You're not invited, then," said Glenn without thinking. Ashley just smiled at him... and suddenly they were the only two people in the world.

And then Craig was there again. "Wanna come out to dinner with us?"

She turned toward him. "Now?"

"Yeah."

"I—I'm sorry. I have things I have to do."

"I could go for a pie," said Craig. "Blueberry, maybe?"

Ashley let out a flustered laugh. "Don't hold your breath. But you know where that bowl goes when you're done."

"Garbage?"

She scoffed in amusement and moved toward the door, which Glenn was still holding. Her hand rested on his forearm. "Keep him straight, will you? And don't be a stranger." She gave him that smile again, her eyes wide and welcoming, and then she was gone.

Glenn let go of the door. It swung shut on its automatic hinge. Craig, swallowing a mouthful of cookie, looked up at him. "See, this is the good floor."

"You know her?" Glenn asked.

"Somewhat."

Glenn sidled up to the table and looked at the cookies. "You... interested in her?"

"Well. She's nice, but... meh."

"Not your type?"

Craig shook his head. "Doesn't... excite me."

Good. Glenn hardly knew Craig, but he got the sense that his new roommate had no trouble getting women. Glenn wasn't certain that he wanted Ashley—certainty takes time—but he did want to become better acquainted with her.

Craig tapped Ashley's plastic bowl. "I'll let you take this back when it's empty. She's at the end of the hall."

Glenn smiled. "Excellent. Now can we please go? I need some real food."

Craig's eyes widened; he stood up immediately. "The last thing I want is to get you angry... Bruce."

Glenn smiled as he remembered the remark. Craig never had gotten him angry, but then... Glenn did not anger easily anyway. His feelings ran deep and strong, but there was usually no point in inflicting them upon others. He could usually understand, and accommodate, other points of view. It didn't mean changing his mind; he simply recognized that others had valid reasons for their opinions and thus should be respected. So he did, and "Bruce" rarely got angry. Football had been a good way to release pent-up emotions, but he didn't have that any more. So... how did he let his feelings out?

Well... Glenn realized at that moment that he didn't know.

"What're you thinking about?" Eric called from the couch. He had apparently been watching.

Glenn thought for a few seconds. "Moving day."

"That was like, months ago... right?"

Glenn looked at him. "Sure." He started to wonder what drug was currently coursing through Eric's system. Then his phone chimed at him.

Check sashas room shes busy! He could almost hear

Craig shouting those words at him. And as much as he would have liked to sit there and imagine what hijinks his roommate was currently getting into... he had to go and check. Someone had taken Ashley... and, thanks to the blizzard, the list of suspects was remarkably small.

He left without a word to his guest.

6

Craig set down his phone on the bathroom counter and looked at himself in the mirror. He looked... sweaty, yes, but also exhilarated. He wasn't just having sex in a pitch-black room with a girl who thought he was Glenn. He was doing it with Sasha—finally! And, accordingly, it was the best sex he'd ever had. Judging from the sounds she had been making, it was pretty damn awesome for her, too. And he wasn't ready for it to end just yet, but he wanted to text Glenn and... frankly... he needed to catch his breath.

Craig turned on the faucet, splashed a little water on his face and smiled at his reflection. He had to be careful not to say anything, because his voice sounded nothing like Glenn's. Sasha had tried to trick his roommate into bed with her... and until he knew why, he intended to keep her in the dark.

He turned off the bathroom light, opened the door and slowly made his way back to the bedroom.

"Welcome back," cooed Sasha, not bothering with the accent any more. Craig paused near the bed, and suddenly he felt her lips wrapping around... it. Oh yes... part two was going to be fun.

Once things had heated up again, it occurred to him that he didn't have protection. Oh well.

The hallway was empty, naturally. At one point, Glenn might have heard a feminine voice yelling, faintly... but blamed it on his imagination.

He knocked on Sasha's door firmly, trying to sound confident even though he didn't know what he'd say if someone answered. No one did. He knocked again, harder. Still no answer. Well... Craig had said she was "busy," so... Glenn grasped the doorknob and gently turned. It was unlocked. He pushed the door open, slowly and quietly as possible. The lights were on, literally, but no one appeared to be home. "Sasha...? Sasha's roommate...?" Unhappy with the sound of his voice, he desperately tried to infuse it with some confidence. "I came to finish what I... started."

He stepped inside and let the door close behind him. He strode purposefully into the bedroom, in case Sasha was waiting for him. She wasn't... and he was almost disappointed. Instead, there was an overly full laundry basket, which he nearly tripped over. The sheer... pinkness of the bedroom was overwhelming without Sasha to distract him. It looked like something out of a children's catalog—the kind of bedroom a little girl would fantasize about having. Usually these girls would grow up and embrace reality. But... he tried not to judge too harshly.

The prescription bottle was still on the desk. Glenn went straight for it—Valium, prescribed to Sasha Goldsmith by someone named "M. Goldsmith." Interesting. "Take as needed," the label said. He assumed the pills inside were indeed Valium, since he had never seen Valium before. After a moment of arguing with himself, he stuffed the bottle in his pocket and moved on to the drawers.

The bottom drawer, of course, contained Sasha's impressive stock of liquor, as well as several bottles of over-the-counter pain relievers and a couple bottles of cough syrup.

Glenn was not the most sexually active man in the world, nor the kinkiest... but he was pretty sure he recognized most of the toys in the middle drawer, although it looked like someone had dropped a pair of needle-nose pliers in there as well. There was also a disheveled pile of condoms—all colors, styles and sizes—at least a dozen. Plus a couple bottles of lubricant... one was even strawberry-flavored.

"As needed," Glenn muttered.

The top drawer didn't live up to his expectations—just school supplies. It seemed a bit strange, though, for Sasha to have two packs of thick, black markers... the kind that give off a really strong smell. Odd, but not what he was looking for.

What was he looking for, again?

Ashley, dumbass.

He looked under the bed and in the closet—nothing. He almost tripped over the heaping laundry basket on his way to the bathroom... no Ashley there, either. He checked the larger of the kitchen cupboards, and then the vacant right side of the suite. No Ashley.

Craig had had reached the peak of his sexual Mount Everest. Twice. In fact, he felt as though he had expended enough energy to scale a mountain... but climbing never felt so good. And despite the fact that Sasha was still moaning and trembling and that all he wanted to do was collapse and sleep... he jumped off the bed, grabbed his clothes from the floor and ran for the door. He had reached the stairwell before realizing that he was still naked, so, he hurriedly pulled on his jockey shorts and continued to the fourth floor. He felt like a superhero speeding back to his secret hideout.

As Glenn left Sasha's apartment, he started to wonder if she'd had anything to do with Ashley's... condition... at all. Perhaps Sasha was just being her usual unpredictable self. Not healthy... but not necessarily illegal, either.

Searching her place, wondering if she would walk in the door at any moment, had made him sweat a little. He moved toward the elevator, slowly and thoughtfully, and pushed the UP button. It did not open immediately.

He heard the stairwell door opening, sensed movement, and turned. Sasha stepped out, wearing only her bra and panties, holding the rest of her clothes in her hand. Her long limbs shiny with sweat, her hair tangled and flat. "There you are," she purred.

Crap. How could he explain being on the second floor? His mind labored for a moment... then he realized that Sasha was staring at him with unbridled lust.

"You look so composed... and I'm a mess! And it's all your fault. You love it, don't you?"

Glenn almost shrugged... but she clearly didn't care that he was on her floor for no apparent reason. So, he simply gave her a sly smile.

She moved in close enough to kiss him. He could smell her sweat, but also a hint of perfume. Her free hand snaked around and squeezed his ass. "Well, here's a secret... I love it, too."

And Glenn felt it. She was inches away; her skin so smooth, her eyes so bright... her lips, looking more succulent than ever... he wanted her.

He closed the space between them and kissed her,

firmly but not forcefully. His hands were on her waist... then her ass. She mirrored his passion with a moan.

They parted after several seconds. "Don't get me started," she said. "I'll do you right here."

She moved away, toward her apartment, with a smile. Glenn, watching her go, realized *he* was fully started. Most days, Sasha exuded sexuality, but in this moment... she *was* sex.

She turned toward Glenn as she opened her door. "Want some more?"

More what? Just go with it. "Now?"

"I'm all warmed up."

Glenn looked around awkwardly. He couldn't... not now... could he? He wanted it... his body did, at least... but somehow it seemed wrong. "I don't think I have it in me."

Sasha smiled. "You're right. It's in me." She winked.

Glenn probably should have smiled, but he didn't. She watched him, expectant, and when no smile came, a bit of concern trickled across her face. "You're not thinking about her, are you?"

Glenn merely narrowed his eyes in response; he was afraid to say anything.

Sasha tossed her clothes into her suite and moved back toward Glenn. "Daisy Duke?" She asked in her laughable accent. "The southern belle?"

Glenn wasn't thinking; he didn't have to. "I'm sorry," he muttered.

She surged forward and took his hands in hers. "It's okay! It's okay!"

He just stared. Her gentleness had stunned him into silence.

"She liked you, it was plain as day! And yet you clearly have a lot of pent-up energy. What's that about? Huh? If she cared about you, why would she keep you from expressing that?"

Glenn stared into her wide, passionate eyes. His facial

muscles were starting to contort involuntarily. "I have to go," he said, pulling away from her. The elevator had arrived while they were talking; he pressed the UP button again and the doors opened. He stepped inside, not looking back.

As the doors closed, Sasha yelled, "You're better than her!"

The elevator moved upward, but not for long. Glenn pushed the STOP button and leaned back against the wall. He couldn't hold back the tears any more.

Craig had chugged a bottle of water from Chuck's fridge and then jumped into the shower. He started with warm water just above body temperature, then inched the H knob down until the stream was pleasantly cool. He had never burned that much energy at once, even in any of his sporadic visits to the gym. In reality, Sasha was, well, crazy... or, as a Psychology major would say, maladaptive. In bed, however, she was... impressive. Craig had bedded a half dozen women, but none with the sheer prowess and body control of Sasha Goldsmith. Part of him wished that he had given in and fucked her months ago. He was sure he could have, but... somehow it hadn't felt quite right yet. He wanted to let the tension build. For some reason he had lied and told Glenn that they had done it... mainly to keep up his reputation, even though he was pretty sure Glenn wouldn't care. Others might.

He did not regret finally doing it now, even though Glenn probably would disapprove. Hell, Glenn had apparently done it himself, so he was now in no position to judge. It had been worth it—the best sex he'd ever had. And judging from her reactions, she had loved it too. Only one thing bothered Craig: Sasha didn't know it was him. Glenn would get the credit for taking her to those intense peaks. And that loose thread, when pulled, gave way to more problems. Why would Sasha masquerade as Ashley? How did she gain the use of Ashley's phone and suite? Ashley would not have approved, and if he remembered correctly, she had planned on staying in the dorm over Thanksgiving. So... where was she?

Sasha and Ashley had never hated each other, as far as he knew, but they had never been friends, either. He couldn't see them conspiring together. Ashley's absence combined with Sasha's deception made him very suspicious. Couple that with what Glenn had been saying... and something was definitely going on.

He heard the apartment door open. No problem; only Chuck and Glenn knew he was staying here, and Chuck was gone until Sunday. He could vaguely make out Glenn's outline through the shower curtain as his roomie walked into the bathroom.

And then—holy shit—Glenn was pulling open the curtain—not just a little, all the way. Craig was surprised, but he didn't hide himself; he wasn't the one trying to look at another guy's junk.

But Glenn was already turning away, almost angrily, it seemed. "What did you do?" Glenn asked from the doorway.

Craig stared at the back of his roommate's head. "Sasha." He turned off the water; he was done anyway.

Glenn sighed.

"I knew it was her... even though she had it dark."

Glenn remained still, facing out into the apartment. "How?"

Craig felt the smartass rising within him. "Closed the shades, turned off the lights, you know..."

Glenn turned to face him, not smiling, but... he didn't look angry, either.

Craig did smile. He held out his hand, toward a towel hung on the wall nearby. He could have reached it himself... but he didn't want to. Instead he held out his hand and, after about five seconds, Glenn grabbed the towel and handed it to him. "I've driven through that tunnel before," Craig said.

Glenn stared blankly at the closest wall as his roommate patted himself dry.

"Wasn't the first time I took a dip in that pool," said Craig. Lying without even thinking, perhaps because Glenn's audacious entrance had annoyed him. He stared until Glenn reluctantly met his gaze. "Did you swim in the deep end too?"

Glenn scoffed and left the room, shutting the door forcefully behind him.

"Come on, man," Craig called after him. "It's fun, but probably a little overrated..." Glenn declined to answer... but he didn't hear the apartment door, so he continued. "Hey, I can't resist her any more than you can!"

It must have been at least five seconds before Glenn's voice came through the door: "And she thought you were me?"

"In case you haven't noticed, you and I do have similar builds... we've got the stubble... and now our hair is the same. We're like twins! In the dark."

"She seemed pretty impressed with your performance."

Craig wrapped the towel around his waist and stepped out into the bedroom. "Wasn't a performance... it was just me." He began to pull off the towel—slowly—and Glenn, taking the hint, stepped out into the living area. "You're welcome, by the way."

"Mmm," came Glenn's reply.

Craig pulled on a clean pair of jockey shorts. He thought of Sasha, trembling... and they got tighter. "She is wild, isn't she?"

"I can't argue with that," said Glenn.

Craig hadn't eaten much since breakfast; his stomach

had started to feel like it was running on empty. He stepped into the living area. Glenn was staring at the digital clock on top of the TV. "They could be here in forty minutes," said his roommate. Craig continued toward the kitchen—the cops were coming? Good. They could figure everything out. The Thanksgiving weekend could continue. And he could help himself to some sliced turkey...

Glenn continued: "We have to find her."

Craig stopped to think for a moment, then opened the refrigerator. Glenn had never seemed so... driven. He wondered what his roomie had seen, what would make him behave this way. "You're sure something happened to her?"

"Of course. Otherwise I'd be sitting down to watch this," said Glenn, gesturing at the TV. *The Searchers* was playing.

Craig nodded, taking out the turkey, the cheese, the mayo. Sasha's deception had convinced him that something was amiss. She was often unpredictable, but rarely underhanded. If Sasha wanted someone in bed, she'd simply ask them... and usually they would say yes. But the police were coming... and Craig did not feel like playing detective at the moment. He had just had the best sex of his life, and now his body wanted only to eat something and fall asleep. On another day, he might have enthusiastically investigated. But not today. "I think you should relax. Sit down for a minute. You want a sandwich?"

Glenn shook his head.

"I'll make you a sandwich," Craig said anyway. After all, everyone loves turkey. "Now hear this. It's a little technique for getting your mind off something you can't change. I learned it from a shrink." He gave Glenn his *this is serious business* look. "No, wait, I figured it out on my own." Didn't he? "Actually, I... I don't remember. But who cares? It works!"

Glenn was staring at him, arms crossed. "It works?"

Craig nodded, reaching for the bread. "Much of the time, it works." He opened the bread bag and pulled out four slices. "First, you picture yourself in your head. Just as you are now."

"You're asking too much."

"Shut it. Now... you envision yourself reaching into your own head and pulling out a photograph."

"Of what...?"

"A photo of whoever or whatever you're trying to get off your mind. You take that photo and put it in your back pocket. It can't bother you there."

"So you could say I'm putting it on... the back burner."

"In your case, literally!"

Glenn lifted one hand toward Craig, middle finger extended. Craig simply beamed at him. "I don't know where you get this stuff, man," Glenn was saying.

"Listen," Craig said. He was running out of arguments; getting closer to his real feelings. He could only think of one word at a time now, so they came out slowly. "Ashley disappeared, or something, right? We could just screw it up worse if we try to find her. Someone... could get... hurt."

Glenn gave him such a look that Craig touched his face to ensure he hadn't grown a second nose. "Since when are you worried about getting hurt?"

"It's not me..." Craig tried to reason. "Ashley, or you, or who knows who else..."

"Bull. You just don't care about her."

Craig looked down and clenched his fist against the counter. "I do, it's just... we're not detectives, Glenn! We're not going to figure this out."

Glenn sighed. "Of all the people who live here, I was sure that I could depend on you for help." He took a few steps forward, and Craig almost mistook the intensity in his eyes for aggression. He continued past the kitchen and opened the apartment door. "You are not a coward. Quit acting like one."

And Glenn was gone.

Craig sighed and looked at the TV. "That'll be the day," said John Wayne.

June 4th... a Thursday.

Craig had the dorm's gym all to himself. Not a spectacular gym... it was basically a converted apartment suite, but it had enough to satiate the fitness-minded. One half devoted to treadmills, bikes, and a few weight machines, the other half—free weights. That was Craig's side. The machines seemed like half-measures to him. He had always been pretty fit naturally, but now he wanted to be... an impressive male specimen. He had also wanted to play football in high school, but dad had not allowed that. No...

Well, Craig was in charge of himself now. Summer had just begun, and he wanted to start something new, something good. He had looked up the basic techniques of weight lifting on the internet. The first session had been tough. The second session had been... tougher. The third session—this one—seemed a little easier, thank God. And he had already noticed an improvement in the size and definition of his muscles... probably not enough for others to notice, but encouraging still. The televisions—one on each end of the gym—made things easier by taking his mind off his muscles. The near one was tuned to a classic movie station currently playing *The Searchers*, a damn good movie. Maybe a little dated, style-wise, but still classic. And Craig could think of no better male role model—or father figure—than John Wayne.

He was finishing his second set of deep squats when

she walked in—a new girl. She was pretty in a doll-like way, and a little shorter than average for a girl. Her modest gym clothes made it difficult to assess her body; he could only tell that she wasn't overweight. She didn't seem to care about appearance—no obvious makeup, and her dark blond hair was tied back in a messy ponytail. She looked around briefly, then hopped onto the nearest treadmill; she had come here to work.

Craig continued to watch her as he guzzled down several mouthfuls of water. Despite the valiant efforts of the air conditioning, he could feel the humidity seeping in from outside. He didn't feel like he could do another set, but he would anyway... three seemed like a good number to do. And he couldn't wimp out now, not with a lady present. He added another fifty pounds almost without thinking, but not without glancing over to see if she was watching. It appeared she wasn't... but there *were* mirrors everywhere...

He took the weight onto his shoulders—it was so heavy that his squat was almost involuntary. Okay, this wasn't too bad... now to rise into a standing position... Craig huffed and he puffed... he felt like something in him was going to burst... but slowly, he was able to rise. His anguished expulsion of breath at the top caused the new girl to glance over, startled. Yeah, now he had her attention. Now to perform another repetition. The squatting down was easy... but only with an immense amount of straining, pushing and grunting could he raise the weight again. She didn't look over this time. *Oh well, try harder*. Starting the third rep, Craig was beginning to think he had gotten the hang of it. He pushed and he strained and—his stomach heaved. Muscles seized up without his permission and the water shot up out of his gullet. He heard the weights hit the floor and realized he had let go of them. The heaving was as exhausting as the squats themselves.

White Friday

After seconds that felt like minutes, the heaving stopped. Craig felt himself running across the room, and then slamming the bathroom door behind him. Multicolored spots were blooming in his vision. Acid was burning in his throat. Worst of all was the heat spreading across his face and head... the girl had seen everything. Right now she was probably shaking with silent derisive laughter.

Craig stumbled to the lone sink and spit, over and over again, trying to get rid of the unpleasant substances that should have stayed in his stomach. How... could this happen? He rarely got sick. He felt fine now... although he was starting to notice some extra soreness in his legs and core. He leaned against the wall and let himself tremble for a few seconds.

A girlish voice penetrated the door, smooth and lilting with a Southern accent. "Everything okay in there?"

Craig tensed up and exploded into coughs. "Sonofa—bitch," he choked out.

"Are you all right?" came the voice.

Craig forced himself to relax—breathe—and the coughing died down. He considered his options... she probably wasn't going to give up. "I'll be fine," he croaked, "if you don't tell anyone about this."

No response for several seconds. He was about to repeat himself when the voice returned—"Well, I might. You don't know me; how can you take my word?"

Normally, he might have thought she was flirting... but this was not the time. And he didn't want to meet any woman who considered vomiting a turn-on. But this one seemed sincere. "You're gonna have to open the door and talk to me," she added, sounding a little amused.

Craig sighed. He didn't feel like it, but he couldn't let her concern go unacknowledged. He rinsed out his mouth, ran a paper towel over his face... then slowly opened the door. There she was, a few steps away, looking up at him. Close up, the light lines on her rosy face made her look closer to 30 than 20.

"So... what's your name?" he asked.

"Ashley. What's yours?"

"Craig."

"You haven't been lifting weights for very long, have you?"

"About... a month," he lied, not wanting to look like a *total* amateur.

"Well, this thing is more common than you might think," she said, sounding rather clinical. "You were just pushing yourself too hard."

Craig pushed the door open the rest of the way. "You... lift?"

"Yeah, can't you tell?" She grinned. So did he. "I've known people... who do. And it happens."

Craig gazed off over her shoulder, eyes unfocusing. He had never heard of this. But then, he had mostly just skimmed the workout directions online.

"So you tried a little too hard," she said with a gentle smile. "Big deal, right?"

"Yeah... I'm intense."

"Sure thing." Her smile was growing more confident now. "And even if I were to tell anyone, if they know you, they'll think nothing of it."

Craig smiled involuntarily. "True..."

"Feel any more coming?"

"No." He now felt as if nothing had happened.

"Good! Just take it easy for a bit."

Craig leaned against the door frame... he had never known a college girl who acted like this. "It's still embarrassing," he said sheepishly.

"Oh, let it go," said Ashley. "You know, I used to be embarrassed of my accent, and I tried to hide it."

Craig stared for a moment, speechless. That gentle lilt may have been the best thing about her. "That's... crazy."

"Thanks," she said with another confident grin. She returned to her treadmill. Craig grabbed a handful of paper towels and started wiping up the liquid he had deposited on the floor. It disgusted him, and yet... she didn't seem to think less of him, so... he wiped it up, and that was that. Ashley called over to him: "Also, a girl doesn't care how much you're lifting, as long as you're making an effort."

Wonderful.

Sasha came in a few minutes later wearing booty shorts and a tiny sports bra, both so tight they looked uncomfortable. She gave Craig a long look, then hopped on a treadmill and started at a sprint.

Craig liked Ashley a lot. Throughout June and July, he had flirted with her at every opportunity, as he did with many of the girls around here. She had almost always returned his attention in her kind yet pragmatic way... and maybe there had been a glimmer of interest. But eventually Craig had realized that although he liked Ashley in many ways, romantically was not one of them. Glenn, on the other hand, had clearly been entranced by her from the start. Over the first few months of the semester, they had interacted regularly, and Craig had silently rooted for them to get together. Glenn, after all, did not flirt with just anyone. And Ashley's flirting with him had seemed more jovial somehow. As he chewed on his turkey sandwich—heavy mayonnaise—he pondered this. Glenn probably cared about Ashley more than anyone else on campus. He had never seen his roommate this energized, but he would probably react that way if something had happened to her.

Craig stuffed the last bite of the sandwich into his mouth and went to finish dressing.

7

Sasha Goldsmith: Daddy's Little Girl. 'Little' because, despite being tall for a girl, she would apparently always be five inches shorter than him. 'Daddy's' because he owned her, a fact that he demonstrated as often as possible. Did mom know? Probably; she had started prescribing sleep aids for Sasha when she was in the 6th grade... and thank God for that. Not because she didn't love her Daddy, but because she *had* started to develop insomnia around that time.

The push-up bra was chafing; she pulled it off and flung it toward her bedroom. Glenn had used his mouth to full effect in the pitch-black room and some areas were still very tender. Too bad there were no boys around to see her topless, but... Hell, she was tired. And sweaty. Too tired to do anything about the sweat. She thought about what she had done and what he had done to her. She giggled. Success! Guys *were* easy to sway, even uptight ones like Glenn.

She spoke to her empty suite: "Why are the quiet ones always so wild in bed? Huh?!" She let out a titter that grew into a full-blown belly laugh. "Seriously!" Glenn—YES, THAT GLENN—had just given her two of the most unexpectedly amazing... *experiences*... she'd ever had. She had lain on the bed, spasming, for at least a minute before realizing that he'd gone. Only one other man had done that to her. The undisputed master.

Physically, Glenn was fine... just fine. Good hair, broad shoulders, in decent shape and just tall enough to meet her standard. The epitome of average. But he rarely spoke to her, and she had never seen so much as an ounce of emotion from him... except a laugh now and then. Usually with Craig, who, let's face it, had his own issues. One time she had found herself alone in an elevator with Glenn while wearing only a towel. Aside from a cursory head-bob when she entered, he had ignored her completely. Usually in that situation she would get stares or pick-up attempts; those things she could work with. But what kind of man would ignore an attractive, scantily-clad female in close quarters like that? Not to mention such an obvious opportunity for elevator sex? She had never known anyone who would turn down elevator sex. Anyway, that was when she had started to suspect Glenn was gay. About a month later, she had glimpsed Glenn walking down the hall past her suite, so she decided to give him another try, just to be sure. She stripped down to bra and panties and stood in her doorway until he passed by again on his way back. "Hey, hon," she had said. "Could you do me a favor? I could really use a massage... and you look like you have good hands..." Glenn had looked her firmly in the eyes, his gaze never falling, and said, "I'm not good at those. Sorry." Then he was gone.

Sasha wasn't an idiot; one rejection might have been a fluke, but two formed a pattern. Glenn was either gay, or he had some sort of weird fetish, like an attraction to horses or fish or... inanimate objects, who the hell knew?

White Friday

She had told her friend Liz about her theory. Liz had probably told a few other people, and it had undoubtedly spread as those juicy tidbits tend to do. Only then had she noticed Glenn flirting, very openly, with Ashley in the stairwell. Then Craig had mentioned, during one of their encounters, that Glenn had a crush on Ashley. Yeah, right. The most boring girl in the building. And conveniently, it had only become apparent AFTER the gay theory had been spread. Sasha had her doubts. The straight men she couldn't seduce were few and far between.

Then had come Thanksgiving and the business with Ashley. Sasha had made a big mistake in giving Eric a hint regarding her plan. He had turned against her. It was probably just temporary, but... Sasha needed someone—a reasonably attractive male with some stamina. She was just in that mood right now, what Daddy liked to call her "fuck everything that moves" mood. He was right, but... did he have to use that ugly word so much? Sure, she would throw around that word during the throes of passion... if a guy got her excited enough... but to her, she was making love. So what if there was no actual love involved—the act itself was a beautiful thing, a lovely thing, and sometimes it could even generate love. She was pretty sure of that, despite a lack of evidence. It *had* to be true; how could two (or more) people come together like that and *not* end up feeling attached to each other? Sex meant love. And her Daddy certainly loved her. But he wouldn't be around forever... and she probably wouldn't be allowed to marry him anyway. So there would have to be another. Maybe several others. Whatever.

But she had been in her "make love to everything that moves" mood and as far as she knew, Glenn and Eric were the only men still in the building. With Eric against her, Glenn was the only option. She would give 110% effort to seduce him and if he really was gay, perhaps she could convince him to "experiment." It actually didn't take that much work at all, and when she felt that lump in his jeans, she knew she had won. Of course, he had won, too, because guys who made love with Sasha Goldsmith always wanted more. They didn't always get it, though.

Just when she had relaxed and settled in for what she expected to be a long session of lovemaking... he had rejected her and walked out. Yes, she had given him the ultimatum—now or never—that she always gave when she felt rejected... but she had needed it badly. She had needed HIM, because Eric had been out of the question. And she had learned that, yes, Glenn did have feelings for Ashley. Then she had found Ashley's phone, and her suite unlocked. And suddenly she had known how to get the loving she needed.

It worked. Glenn had shown up and rocked her world. She had never expected such a reserved guy to know so many positions and techniques. Sure, quiet guys had surprised her in the past, but never so overwhelmingly. She didn't know if Glenn had realized her true identity in that dark room and she didn't care. Their 45-minute session had qualified as 'fucking.' Why? Because it had been fucking awesome, and well worth any foreseeable consequences, including another abortion, if needed.

Sasha had seen afterward, in the hall, that Glenn still had some unresolved feelings toward Ashley. That was unfortunate for more than one reason. Oh well. She was well on her way to loving him—the guy she had previously written off as boring and gay.

He would come back sooner or later. They both would, actually. And she would choose Glenn, because Eric did not appreciate what she had tried to do for him. Perhaps having been with so many women had spoiled him. She felt that Glenn, however, would give her the appreciation she deserved. She couldn't really say why. In the meantime, though, she had reading material.

Glenn's lovemaking had forced Sasha to hold onto Ashley's mattress for dear life several times. At one point, her fingers had slipped under the mattress... and touched the spine of a book. After Glenn had run off and she had... finished, she had put on her underwear, pulled out the book and wrapped it in the rest of her clothes. Now she pulled it out, a simple yet dignified leather-bound journal, the cover and spine lightly worn from use. In the top margin on the first page was the name *Ashley Freeman*, printed in neat, boxy letters with blue ink. Sasha read the first line below it: *Dr Bethune says it might help to keep a therapy journal, so... here goes!*

This could be very enlightening.

Someone had to keep an eye on the uninvited guest in their suite... and Glenn supposed it had to be him. After all, his roommate was much too busy being comfortable... away from him. Well, fine. Time to find some new friends, perhaps. Anyway, he had searched Sasha's suite... where could Ashley's body be? And... who else could have taken her? He didn't know anyone who had stayed for the weekend, beyond Eric, Sasha and Craig. He needed to sit and think.

Eric was stretched out on the couch, and Glenn had never seen him looking so relaxed and... unfettered. He was still watching the same channel that Craig had been watching.

"*Searchers*?" Glenn asked, approaching.

"You know it, pilgrim," Eric drawled.

Glenn smiled... he almost liked him in that moment. For once, he wasn't gazing around a room trying to pick up on the conversations of others, or looking for the attention of any attractive girls in the area. He was just... enjoying life. Eric, he decided, could be eliminated... as a suspect, he thought with a chuckle. He had been here, in

Glenn's apartment, for the most part. He had, apparently, gone back to his own place for a beer and... who knows what else... but it seemed he had been here, relaxing, the rest of the time. Given his current state of 'relaxation,' perhaps brought on by some mystery substance, it seemed unlikely that he'd pull a complicated stunt like hiding a body. So, Eric was not a suspect. And that made things a little bit easier... but it also tightened the noose a bit. There were four living people in the building (that he knew of). Taking himself out of the pool left two... the same two that had been cavorting in Ashley's bedroom earlier. Could they have...?

Glenn didn't want to believe it. But, he considered Craig's behavior—specifically his unwillingness to search for Ashley—and he reluctantly began to suspect.

"I am thinking about talking to Ashley," he said.

Eric slowly turned toward him, as if coming out of a trance. "So you're listening to me now?"

Glenn felt a little warmth in his cheeks. "Well, I... like her. And, I guess it's like they say, the time is now..."

Eric picked up his beer bottle, shook it, and saw that it was empty. "The time is always now."

"I just can't find her. And I'm worried." Glenn set his jaw and waited for Eric's response.

Eric glanced toward the floor, then the TV. Glenn was beginning to feel uncomfortably warm. "I'll find her," said Eric finally. "But you have to ask her out. Today." He looked Glenn squarely in the eye, as if to indicate he had no hope of backing out.

Glenn swallowed hard. He already felt like a manipulator... but this was worse. Ashley was gone, and he would not be asking her out... ever.

His face must have looked ashen, because Eric reacted to him with mild disgust. "Don't be a pussy." He picked up his cell phone and called a stored number. "I told you, women are mere mortals like us..." He listened quietly for a bit, expecting an answer, then ended the call. "Three rings, no voicemail. Let's see if she's home."

"Okay," said Glenn flatly. He wasn't looking forward to this, but Eric could prove useful. And he hated the idea of using someone... even Eric... but he needed help. He was flailing.

As he stood, Eric said, "You know, I've had a few beers, but I don't really feel—" He instantly stumbled and caught himself on a chair. "Whoa, there it is!"

Craig stood at a crossroads. The foyer was ahead, the main stairwell behind. On his left and right, the main hall that comprised the backbone of the E-shaped building. He gazed out through the glass front doors... everything was white. He wasn't in Canton anymore... obviously. The mountains were similar, but the weather up here was something else.

He wondered what dad was doing right now, besides waiting for retirement. Harold Flynn was a committed man—he would follow through on what he started. He wouldn't let things like difficulty or lack of interest stop him... but he would make life miserable for everyone around him if he hated his job. Which he did.

Some would say he consistently raised a bigger stink than the paper mill he worked in, but he was the most dependable and versatile worker in the plant, and the managers knew it. The major difference between home and work was that, well... he had never hit anyone at work. Craig himself had wanted to hit Glenn twice today already, and that was not an urge that his roomie aroused in him often. The violence, though... that was a relic of his interactions with Harold. There is no good excuse for a father to bully his son. Craig had grown tired of it by age thirteen. He realized that he could hit his father back... followed closely by the realization that

Harold would simply hit back as well. Harder. So, Craig took his father's abuse... mostly verbal, but occasionally physical... he learned to become a parrot: "Yes, sir, that mill *does* sound like a shithole" and "Yes, sir, you *were* dealt a shitty hand in life"... and anger gathered inside him. He fantasized about punching out his old man and kicking him when he was down. And when anyone near his size disrespected him, he didn't hold back. In 10th grade, he broke a 12th-grader's jaw... but that wasn't the jaw he had wanted to break. The fallout from that incident was enough to convince Craig that he should at least *try* to control himself. So, he held it back... most of the time.

Mary Flynn, the woman he had once called his mother, had always been perfectly obedient to Harold. Had never complained or disagreed or stood up for herself or her son in any way. Little Craig's tearful pleadings failed to sway her, as long as Harold consistently brought home the checks that paid for cigarettes and cable TV. And he did. "A committed man is hard to find, darling," Mary would say. "Perhaps you'll understand that when you're older. We could do a lot worse than your father."

Craig got his first job as soon as someone would hire him—a sixteen year-old spending his summer months working at a cemetery. The head groundskeeper was a middle-aged goof-off named Jerry who liked to say, "You won't last long putting people in the ground if you don't have a good sense of humor!" The same was true for living in an abusive household. Craig's class clown tendencies and developing good looks made him popular with the majority of the high school crowd. And he fielded come-ons from many of the most attractive girls in school, but he would not tolerate any girl who allowed herself to be mistreated or taken advantage of by a man. It happened in high school more often than one might think. In his own mind, he had already disowned his mother for her permissive attitude toward Harold; no woman with similar tendencies would be allowed to stay in his life. No... he would rather be with someone so fiercely independent that she could leave him at any time. Someone with a will of her own. And although he refused to tolerate Mary any longer, he didn't blame her. He blamed his father.

Craig closed his eyes. He visualized himself reaching into his head, pulling out a picture of Harold and sliding it into his back pocket. Now he could focus.

As he sauntered down the west wing hall, he found another person emerging in his mind: Sasha. He had fucked her, finally, after all the flirting, arguing, threatening... the tension had broken and the storm had raged. He had always wanted her, not just because of her unrelenting sexuality nor her notoriety, which reached far beyond Tomlin University. He wanted her because of the way she interacted with him. When their personalities met, it was like two bighorn rams crashing against each other at full speed to win dominance. No other woman had ever been brave enough—stupid enough?—to challenge him so fearlessly... and, surprisingly, he loved it. Even more surprisingly, their clashes usually ended in stalemate... and he was okay with that. In fact, he would be okay if that went on for the rest of his life.

Okay, so, Sasha probably still believed that it had been Glenn in that dark bedroom giving her the boning of her life. That could be resolved, though. Truth usually came out sooner or later. And speaking of truth, there was another dangling issue—just how did she get access to Ashley's phone and suite? Yes, Sasha acted strange sometimes, but she had always seduced guys in her own suite. And it was... *possible*... that she and Ashley had worked something out. Possible, but hardly probable. And if they had... *why*?

Craig knocked on the door of room 116, a single apartment in the west wing. It was a crap shoot; he didn't expect them to be here... but he knew wherever they were, they were together.

There was no immediate response. They were probably spending the holiday weekend with family. Just to amuse himself, Craig deepened his voice and shouted "Police Officer!"

At that, he heard a slight stir behind the door. "Open up, please," said Craig in a mock-authoritative tone.

There was movement near the door; perhaps someone looking through the peephole. Then a relieved voice—feminine and sharp. "We're not home, sir!"

Craig put his hands on his hips. "Don't make me get the battering ram."

"Oh dear," said the female voice, faintly. After a moment, a latch clacked and the door swung inward. Cheryl beamed out from behind it—a tall, chubby young woman with glamorous good looks, though she didn't seem to care about accentuating them.

"We got a call about a domestic disturbance, ma'am."

Cheryl raised her eyebrows. "Oh, you mean someone watching the game when he should be doing laundry?"

Craig looked instantly toward the television hanging on the back wall—a football game. "Last night's game?" He stepped past Cheryl into the apartment.

The TV was flanked by two high-quality stereo speakers whose face plates had been removed to allow tinkering. Several large elegant-looking candles burned throughout the place, and white Christmas lights had been strung up along the top of every wall. Sitting on the standard dorm couch facing the TV was Sidney—a fun-looking two hundred and sixty-pound man sporting a shaved head and a Hawaiian shirt. He welcomed Craig with an upraised palm as he approached.

"He downloaded it, as usual," said Cheryl.

White Friday

"I ain't paying for that network," spouted Sid. "That's grand larceny. Football should be on basic cable."

Craig extended a fist and let himself flop into an empty chair. "Preach it, brother!"

Cheryl leaned against the kitchen counter and watched the two men with amusement. "You want something to drink?"

"Beer?" asked Craig hopefully.

"You know us better than that."

"Yeah," said Craig. He did. He had known them for about eighteen months, in fact. Since he had moved into this building. "I actually wanted to ask if either of you have been out of the apartment today."

Sid shook his head, eyes still locked on the screen. "Uh-uh."

Cheryl crossed her arms. "Why?"

Craig was starting to feel a little nervous. He wasn't quite sure what to say. "You haven't... heard anything unusual, in the hall?"

"No..." said Cheryl. "Why?"

It was time for the rubber to meet the road. When it came down to it, Craig really didn't know for sure that anything shady was going on. But he did know that Ashley was missing, that Sasha was acting exceptionally odd, and that Glenn was noticeably upset. And that was enough to make him believe. "We're having some trouble... with Ashley. She's kind of... missing."

This was enough to turn Sid away from the game. "Little Ashley?"

"You don't think she tried to drive in this..." said Cheryl.

"Drive in what?" asked Sid, looking clueless.

Cheryl sighed. "You NEED to pay attention to the outside world now and then."

Craig, feeling awkward, sidestepped the issue as well as he could. "Her car is still here. And I think she'd know better."

Cheryl, looking disturbed, approached the couch and put a hand on Sid's shoulder. He reached over and took her hand, almost instinctively it seemed. "What can we do?" asked Sid.

Craig hesitated, then asked. "How much do you know about Sasha?"

Sid cringed a bit, then looked up at Cheryl, whose eyes had widened. "Too much," she said thickly. "Why do you ask?"

"Well, you are... or were... her roommate."

Cheryl hung her head. Sidney was watching her closely. The football announcers droned on in the background.

"I never knew what that girl was going to be like, from one day to the next... from one *hour* to the next."

Craig climbed out of his chair and gestured toward the dining table. Cheryl smiled, squeezed Sidney's hand and moved in that direction. Once they were seated across from each other, she went on. "She seemed like a lovely person on move-in day... energetic, making jokes, smiling for no reason... a real pleasure. Some time that afternoon she went out for a bit and came back dragging some guy along... I just figured he was her boyfriend... and they went straight into her bedroom. Wasn't two minutes later I started hearing *sounds*..."

"What kind of sounds?"

"The kind of sounds that are none of my beeswax," she replied sharply. "So I came down here to see my man for a while. I was here till around eleven. When I got back, she was just comin' out of her bedroom with a *different* guy."

Craig widened his eyes and pursed his lips, but he wasn't really surprised. He had been around Sasha enough to know that she just got into those moods sometimes... insatiable. Perhaps it would stop once she found the right man. Like... him.

"Now I don't care if she wants to sleep around, as long as she ain't obnoxious about it. Anyway... the next two days, Sunday and Monday, all she did was lay on the couch and stare at the TV. Didn't say a word, didn't leave the suite... and Monday was the first day of classes!"

Craig nodded, looking appropriately concerned. He had seen that side of her, too.

"Still, nothin' I can't live with, but she didn't clean up after herself. I'm talkin' dirty dishes layin' all over, tissues, clothes... the pizza that she ordered and got some guy from down the hall to bring it up to her, she left half of it lay on the table for a week. I let it go at first, but after a while I had to say something. Nicely. I mean, she didn't tell me what was going on, how do I know she didn't just get dumped or something? So I asked her to clean up some of her stuff, and as I was walkin' away, she says something under her breath."

"You heard it?"

Cheryl nodded. "She called me a—" She glanced back toward Sidney, then lowered her voice. "She called me a 'fat fuck.'"

Ouch. Craig closed his eyes. He felt for her... although he himself had been called far worse by Sasha... and he hadn't minded.

Cheryl sat back, folding her arms. "That was the first dent in my patience."

8

Eric was striding down the third floor east hallway, feeling rather confident and pleased with himself. He had presented a good argument. Glenn hadn't liked it—a lot of people don't like to hear the truth. He had rebelled, gone away somewhere to think, and then come back to admit that Eric was right. And he needed Eric's help. Who wouldn't feel confident and pleased in such a situation?

He had gotten his drunk-walk down to a science. Left foot, right foot, and a little extra exertion to make sure he didn't wobble. Beer wasn't the only foreign substance in his system at the moment, but it was the strongest one. And aside from the tendency to wobble, he felt fiiiiiine.

He passed Ashley's apartment at the corner and turned right, toward his own place further down the hall. That's when the voice came from behind him—Glenn's voice. "Hey. I thought we were—"

"I need a beer," drawled Eric, without stopping.

"No you don't."

"Don't tell me what I need," said Eric casually. He knew his own needs, and he did need another cold one.

He needed to keep this buzz going. It was too good to let go.

But the voice behind him persisted. "You've got the rest of the weekend to get drunk off your ass. Or stoned or whatever the hell you do. Try being useful just this once."

Eric stopped and turned, giving Glenn what he thought was a threatening glare. In reality, it was more of a dead-eyed leer, but Eric didn't know that. Glenn just stood there, staring back, not appearing afraid. Fool.

After a few seconds of "glaring," Eric turned and continued toward his place. He sauntered, as smoothly as you could want, down the hall and into his apartment. A small plastic bag lay on the kitchen counter, full of colorful tablets. He paused and looked at them for a moment, then remembered himself and turned toward the refrigerator. He took a bottle of beer from his crisper drawer, twisted off the cap, and swallowed a mouthful. Awesome.

Glenn hadn't moved, nor changed his expression, when Eric got back to him, beer in hand. "That wasn't so hard, was it?" Eric asked slowly. He walked up to Ashley's door, standing closer than a sober person would. He knocked twice, hard enough to make the hanging scarecrows bounce.

Several seconds passed, and he knocked again. "Ashley?"

He sensed Glenn's presence behind him. He had to do something. No answer on Ashley's phone. No answer at her door...

Eric grabbed the doorknob, turned and pushed. The door opened. He stepped inside without a thought.

The suite was dark. Very dark... a combination of blinds and curtains being closed plus the sun being on the other side of the building. But every apartment had two light switches next to the door. He flipped them both up. Light from overhead flooded the entry/dining area and the adjacent kitchen.

"Ashley?" he called. "Sam?" It seemed kind of moot now, since he had already entered, but he wanted to be... what, polite? Something like that.

Nothing had changed since the last time he had been here, about a month ago. Decorative fall leaves, orange and red candles. A rustic-looking coat rack made from a large tree branch—that was Sam's. Their television was small, but then, they rarely used it. Their furniture, however, looked very comfortable with added blankets and pillows. The occupants were both very down-to-earth and likeable, if not exceptionally girly.

Over the first couple months of the semester, Eric had spent much of his time here in the common area, or in Sam's bedroom, off to the right. He had felt more comfortable here than at his own place; the girls had made it that way. He had loved Sam, of course. Ashley, for her part, had been a very gracious host, even if she did spend a lot of time alone in her bedroom.

The place was pretty tidy, as usual, except for several empty water bottles laying around. Two in the living area and one on the dining table—these were the clear, disposable type. Two larger, sturdier, re-usable sport bottles sat on the kitchen counter—one purple, one blue, both empty. Near those sat a water pitcher, the kind that used a replaceable filter. Had Eric been sober, he might have thought it slightly odd for them to leave these things sitting out. Instead he started toward Ashley's darkened bedroom.

Glenn's voice: "Have you been in there before?"

Eric stopped, without turning, and pointed toward the other bedroom. "I've been in Sam's room. Process of elimination leaves this one to be Ashley's." As he stepped into her bedroom, he heard Glenn mumble something sarcastic, but he did not care what it was.

As soon as he turned on the light, he saw that Ashley's bed had not been made. In fact, it looked exceptionally messy. Not that he had been in there before, but it still seemed uncharacteristic for her. Then he noticed a blanket, stuck to the wall with thumbtacks, covering the window. It blocked most of the light from outside. He couldn't say whether Ashley had done that or not. Everyone has a hidden nature, after all; sometimes it's the iceberg... and sometimes it's just the tip.

He emerged from Ashley's bedroom to find Glenn snooping in the refrigerator. "Any clues?" Eric asked, not even trying to hide his sarcasm.

Glenn gave him a quizzical look and pulled out a roasted chicken—whole, untouched, still in its supermarket container. Oh. Eric's heart sank a little. She hadn't touched it...

Eric stared at the chicken for a few moments, disappointed. Then he looked up at Glenn. "Good work, Sherlock." He looked around for a distraction and pointed to the purple sport bottle on the counter. "That's Ashley's bottle, in case you want to swap some spit. Since you can't do it the normal way."

Glenn shoved the chicken back into the fridge and gave him a hurt look. That look... it gave Eric a twinge of regret. Not enough to apologize, though. He turned away... and Sam's bedroom door caught his eye. He stared at it for several seconds.

"Lots of memories in there?" asked Glenn.

"Yeah," Eric shot back. "Because I actually asked her out. And she said yes." He stepped toward the door, put his hand on the knob, turned it gently. It was unlocked, of course. "And we did stuff..."

He stepped inside; the blinds and curtains were open in here, but still, the daylight was weak. He flipped the switch for the overhead light. The bed was a bit messy—that was normal—but everything else remained quite organized. A pair of snowshoes hanging on the wall, a well-used baseball glove on her bookshelf, the ever-present Native American quilt on her bed—some of the hallmarks that made Sam's room unique.

Just looking around, Eric began to feel the beginnings of excitement. He remembered the last time...

October 22nd ...a Thursday.

Sam got up and stormed out of the bedroom. Eric remembered the look she had given him moments before—anger and despair both fighting for control. Perhaps both had won.

He followed her, hurriedly zipping up his pants in case Ashley was around.

"Please, God, tell me you're kidding," came Sam's voice from the kitchen.

"I'm sorry!" he called. "I tried—"

"You said you quit! You said... you were done with that stuff!"

"It's not like I'm shooting up..." A feeble argument, but all he had.

"I don't care! You lied!"

Sam had taken her blue sport bottle out of the fridge and was now swirling water around in her mouth. She refused to look at him. He just watched. Her long black hair swayed as she whirled to spit into the sink. When she finally turned toward him, her brown eyes were wide and watery. Her western-style shirt was still mostly unbuttoned. She had a lovely physique—thin and nicely toned, but not so much as to look muscular, and naturally bronze skin. But right now she was shaking with... rage perhaps... and it was unpleasant for both of them. "I gave you a second chance," she sputtered. "You blew it."

Eric smiled involuntarily. "Nice choice of words."

She glared. "You know how hard I try to put only natural and organic things in my body, and you—"

"Hey! If what you just had wasn't organic, I don't know what is!"

"Get out. It's over."

Whoa. Wait. No. She couldn't mean... what she had said. "What do you mean...?"

"We discussed this. What, did you take some pill and forget?"

Ouch. Eric looked away defensively—he glimpsed the baseball bat that Sam kept in the corner between her bedroom and bathroom. "I... I think we should discuss it again."

"I DON'T DATE DRUG USERS!"

He stared at her; he had never seen her face so red. Her cheeks, twitching. She looked so... vulnerable. Maybe he could...

He leaned forward, slowly. His hands moved toward her shoulders. Once their faces were inches apart, he began to close his eyes and part his lips...

Her fist slammed into his cheek and he staggered, more from shock than the force of the blow. His foot hit the tree-branch coat rack and he stumbled backward, falling. He twisted, desperate not to land on top of that wooden monstrosity... and managed to miss it. Still, he hit the floor pretty hard, and when he finally looked up... Ashley was standing in the doorway.

She stood there frozen, eyes wide, backpack hanging over her shoulder. Eric looked over at Sam. She had crossed her arms and was staring at the wall. "You'd better go," she said stiffly.

Ashley started to back away.

"Not you, Ash," said Sam, softening her tone a bit. "I'm sorry. I mean him."

Eric had gotten to his knees. He wasn't about to take this. Sam had known about his pills since early in their relationship. She had asked him to quit, yes, but... they were in love! What difference did a few pills make? He could quit, probably, but... why? It wouldn't change anything. He was still Eric, Sam was still Sam, and they loved each other. They hadn't said it yet, of course... but *still*... "No."

"Eric!"

Ashley looked like she wanted to back out of the room and never come back. He felt bad for her... but he had to fight for this relationship.

"I didn't do anything wrong!" he cried.

Sam looked him in the eye. "Right," she said quietly. "I forgot, nothing you do is ever wrong." A tear finally sprouted from her eye. "If I have to be wrong, that's fine... I'd rather be happy than right. And I can't be happy with you."

Eric had never felt so close to a girl before. And no girl had ever said anything like that to him. The pain... the loss... was indescribable. All because of an offhand remark...

"Come on. We can..." He was pleading now. But his voice trailed off as Sam stepped toward her room and picked up her baseball bat.

Eric stood up and backed away. He was aching on the inside... but he had seen her swing that thing. He grabbed his satchel from the dining table and backed toward the door. Ashley moved out of his way.

Sam began to relax... then she saw the little bag of pills on the kitchen counter. *His* pills. She picked it up and looked at them for a moment. Then... "Hey."

Eric stopped just outside the doorway.

"Your 'allergy' pills?" Sam's voice had a venomous quality. She flung the bag at him with a pitcher's strength and accuracy. It hit Eric's hand and bounced off into the hall. He watched as she stormed out of the kitchen, and he heard her bedroom door slam.

There was acid in his veins—a cold burning. This felt final. And... humiliating. He reached down for his pills... but next to the bag stood a pair of feet in black, sturdy-looking shoes. Dark blue pants. Oh no.

"Hold up," said a gravelly, mid-range male voice.

Eric straightened up and looked at the officer. He had seen him on campus before; a stocky man, average height. Bald, with glasses and an ambitious mustache. His nametag read **Miller**. "Those yours?"

Eric knew he was screwed. No hope. Still, he had to say something. "I—"

"They're mine," said an unmistakable female voice nearby.

Eric looked to his left... there was Ashley in the doorway, backpack in her hand.

Miller looked at her, just a bit incredulous, then picked up the plastic bag.

"I have a prescription," said Ashley, digging into a side pouch on her backpack. And what she pulled out was, well... a prescription. She handed it to Miller, who read it ravenously.

"Clo-naz-e-pam," Miller pronounced slowly. "That's a sedative, right?"

"It's for lots of things." She said it in such a matter-of-fact yet childlike manner that Miller could only smile and nod politely.

"Shouldn't they be in a bottle?" asked the officer.

"Ohh," said Ashley, a bit bashful. "I don't like the rattling sound. They're... quieter in the baggie."

Miller looked intently at Ashley. She gave him a pleasant smile. After a few moments, he handed her the prescription and the pills. "Be careful with them. And *don't* share them." He glanced at Eric, who could only watch, tense.

"Yes, sir," said Ashley, sounding entirely proper as she stuffed them into her backpack.

White Friday

Miller went on. "I heard you people from down the hall. What's been going on here?"

Eric's cheeks felt like they were glowing. "That'd be me," he said. "I was... getting dumped."

Hearing this, the officer looked from him to Ashley. Her eyes went wide. "Not by me."

Now Miller just looked awkward. "Well, I can understand these things... but people are studying. So try to keep your... domestic disputes... as quiet as possible."

Ashley nodded. Eric imitated her... that was all he could do at the moment. He couldn't think; he could barely breathe. His stash had landed right in front of a police officer... well, campus police, whatever... and he had gotten away with it. It was like... a miracle.

Miller had turned. He was walking away. Eric realized that he needed to exhale, badly. So... after a few seconds of trying to remember how, he just opened his mouth—an out came the flood of air. Without thinking, he turned quickly and wrapped his arms around Ashley. She hugged back briefly then patted him on the back, saying nothing.

By the time Eric released her, he couldn't stop breathing. In and ouuuuuut. In and ouuuuuut. He was enjoying it. He turned toward his place, anticipating a beer or five, which would probably taste better than ever... but a hand had grabbed his wrist.

He looked back... Ashley was tugging him back toward her suite. "Come on," she was saying.

Eric's mind went a little wild and he went with her. He had seen pornos that started this way... not that he was really into Ashley, but he wouldn't say no, especially tonight. Tonight, he just wanted to live, and breathe, and feel.

She got them both drinks, then sat down at the dining table, to the left of the counter that separated them from the kitchen. Eric, after receiving a stern look, decided it best to sit opposite her.

Ashley took a drink from her purple sport bottle as she looked at the plastic baggie full of colorful pills. "These are not allergy pills."

Eric stared blankly, his fingers wrapped around the cold bottled water she had given him. Perhaps she knew that for a fact... perhaps not. But she was smart enough to understand. So he just shook his head.

"And they're not sleeping pills."

"They could be," said Eric. He was hoping that she would either play along, or laugh. She did neither.

"They're not."

Eric dropped his gaze toward the table. She wasn't in the mood for games, apparently... but then, why would she be? After, presumably, a long day of classes, she had walked in on a vicious fight in her own apartment. Then she had put her own ass on the line just to get him out of trouble. It was... amazing.

"Thank you, okay?" Eric spouted. "I almost had the worst luck ever."

Her smile was not entirely humorless. "And who knows when you'll get lucky again?"

Eric flung himself against the back of his chair, almost upsetting it. "God, what is wrong with me?" He opened his water bottle and splashed half of it onto his face. "Why can't I stop?"

Ashley watched calmly, as if the person across from her wasn't completely losing it. "I'm going to reflect that question back at you."

Eric sat silent for several seconds. First he stared at her face, hoping that it might soften and that she might provide the answer for him. But she sat there motionless, and he was forced to think for himself. To get back to the reason for this whole mess, the reason for the pills...

Eric had graduated high school ranked 43rd out of 661. He wasn't a straight-A student, though... more of a

White Friday

"mostly A's, never lower than a B" student. Still, his parents were exceedingly proud. They told everyone they met that their genius son spent five hours every night studying... shut away in his bedroom. Truthfully, Eric was naturally smart enough to earn mostly A's without studying much. He paid attention during class and crammed before tests... and that was enough. He spent most of his "studying" time watching TV and chatting with girls on the internet.

His first major crush came in the fifth grade—a tall girl who had just started to develop. From then on, he'd had about a dozen new crushes each year... the sexy girl in the first row in homeroom, the cute girl who happened to be his lab partner in Chemistry class, the charismatic senior in charge of the yearbook committee, who he loved taking orders from... Eric just loved women. His life revolved around them—looking at them, thinking about them, evaluating them... And every year, he had managed to date one or two of his crushes. These relationships rarely lasted longer than three months, but they were his life. He was ecstatic when they began... but usually both parties ended up losing interest and drifting apart. Easy to start, difficult to maintain. He hadn't worried about it; he figured that when he met "the one," it would just be a perfect relationship and easy to maintain forever.

Eric had entered Tomlin University three years ago looking forward to a major in Criminal Justice; C-J seemed like a noble and somewhat exciting pursuit as well as a great chance to do some good in the world. He had the grades and the aptitude for it, according to everyone who knew him. But... his workload after the first few days of class made him realize that college would require five hours of *actual* studying each night, if not more. And Eric had tried; God knows he had tried... He made it four whole days before he needed a major break—a Thirsty Thursday party and a gorgeous girl named Whitney had provided it. Unfortunately, that "break" had lasted three days, and when he came to his senses, he was already hopelessly behind on classwork. He had tried again; God knows he had tried again. But he simply could not string together more than a few days of honest studying without needing some kind of prolonged stress relief, usually in the form of alcohol and/or female companionship. His natural smarts were just not enough anymore.

On the other hand, his love life—or perhaps one could say his crush life—had gotten along just fine. A tall, athletic Resident Assistant named Beth had caught his eye on move-in day. He had almost pegged her as a lesbian at first, but still he flirted with her regularly, just to see what would happen. Apparently Beth enjoyed his company, for she invited him to a party on a Friday night in October, a party attended mostly by seniors. They all took turns bitching about professors and class requirements over beer. Still, Eric had felt rather out of place, until Beth took him by the hand and led him into her roommate's bedroom, where pills were being distributed among the guests. Pills that looked like colorful antacids.

Eric stared nervously at the orange tablet in his hand. Beth smiled, ran a hand along his stomach and said, "You gotta let loose sometime..."

Sometimes the opposite sex can be a gateway drug.

Eric had spent the rest of that weekend at Beth's place—and much of that time in her bedroom. Athletic? Yes. Lesbian? No way.

He and Beth slept together a few other times that year, though they never officially dated. The pills—known to them as Ex—became much more important to him. By the following spring, he had gotten to the point where he couldn't relax without them. Alcohol and pot were okay as a change of pace, but a lot of work—you had to keep drinking or smoking in order to maintain the effect. Besides, those two drugs made him feel numb, more or less, and calm... but Ex actually provided a positive sensation—a feeling of well-being. Those little pills simply made life... awesome. Of course there were side effects, and as with any drug, they varied depending on the user. The cost of happiness to Eric was mild to moderate dehydration while it was in his system. Some people, including Sasha, felt nauseous after taking it, and a few actually vomited. He had seen those reactions... and, once, an acquaintance of his had died, presumably from taking Ex. The guy simply took two or three pills, drifted into a contented sleep, and never woke up. Not a bad way to die, really... assuming his sleep had been nightmare-free.

After a semester and a half, Eric had decided that Criminal Justice was simply too complex and heavy for him. He searched for a major with less pressure and lower expectations; he found Education. Still, he used Ex at least once day. Beth's roommate had introduced him to a small network of dealers; he met one of them twice a month at the Waffle House near campus. After about a year, he found that he needed a dose of Ex just to fall asleep some nights. He usually woke up feeling dehydrated and dizzy, occasionally nauseous... and once or twice he found himself wishing he could fall asleep and never wake up.

Still, as bad as he felt sometimes, he was fairly certain that he'd feel worse without the Ex.

"Sure," he said finally. "I know why."

"And...?"

"I was misled." This solicited a suspicious look, so he continued quickly. "Look, somehow I got this... this mental image of a world that doesn't exist. You know, a world where you can just be good and treat everyone nice... and you'll be happy?"

Ashley's expression softened a little. "That's... normal. That's how we would like it to be."

"Yeah, but it's not real. You can be good, and treat people well, and still get shit on." He paused for effect; no response from Ashley. "I went to Sunday school, I paid attention, but it doesn't work." Another pause; still no response. "Being nice, being good... doesn't make life good."

"And what does make life good?"

He pointed at the pills. "Those do. Look, someone told me that those things would make life bearable, and they were—"

"Stop it," said Ashley, with an angry expression that actually frightened him. He stopped talking. "No," she said after a few seconds. "The foot thing."

Oh. Yeah. He had gotten a little too worked up, and had thought that maybe she would be open... but no.

Ashley continued, less angry but still intense. "Now, no offense, but you're full of shit."

Eric sat there, stunned. He had never heard her use a curse word. "Come again?"

"We all have... expectations that don't get met. We all have to adjust to... certain aspects of the world."

She wasn't wrong. Eric sat back in his chair, trying to think of a way to turn the discussion back in his favor. He knew he could win. "Well... I wouldn't say that life is nothing but misery. Never. But... there are rough patches. No denying that."

"Mmm," said Ashley.

He waited for more from her. She was staring blankly at the wall behind him, so he continued. "And someone told me that this stuff would make life more bearable. And it does!"

He waited for a retort from Ashley. None came.

"I can take one of those... and suddenly life is a lot more fun. Really, no shit. Pillows feel softer... music has more feeling... and somehow there seems to be more color in the world. I don't know how that works, it just does..."

Ashley was looking him steadily in the eye now, a bit of sadness in her face. He suddenly felt strangely like a car salesman reeling in a customer.

"If you could make your life better just by taking a pill, well... great! Right?"

Ashley glanced down at the pills. She seemed to be stuck in a quandary.

Eric desperately wanted a response now. He wanted to know what she was thinking. Maybe... maybe she would even try Ex. "Wouldn't you sign up for that?"

She finally spoke, quietly. "If they could do that... yes."

Eric exhaled and smiled. He felt... validated.

Ashley continued: "But—"

A door was opening. Sam's door. Shit. Eric grabbed the pills and dropped to the floor, hiding behind the waist-high counter that separated the dining area and kitchen.

"I'm sorry you had to see that." Sam's voice sounded shaky, like she had been crying.

Ashley smiled gently. "No biggie. You okay?"

Sam sniffled. "I don't know. But I will be."

"So it's definitely over?"

He heard Sam take a deep breath—in and out. "He had two chances," she said. "I don't know why I gave him one."

Eric didn't feel so validated anymore.

He ended the remembrance there. It wasn't just bittersweet; it was sweet-bitter-bitter-sweet-bitter. Just thinking of it all was enough to tire him out.

Glenn would probably make a smart remark, any second now. Eric leaned against Sam's door frame, anticipating. He looked around; nothing had changed.

Except... the baseball bat was not in its corner. And... it was nowhere in sight. Hmm. Perhaps she had taken it home until spring.

No sarcastic words had come forth. He stepped toward the kitchen. Glenn was in the living area, looking out the big front windows. "Still snowing," he said quietly.

Eric had seen enough of this place. "Come on," he said, moving toward the door. "There's no reason to be here."

He wanted some more Ex.

White Friday

Excerpts from Ashley's Journal

June 10

Dr Bethune says it might help to keep a journal while I'm in therapy, so... here goes! I don't think I have journaled since 6th or 7th grade! Is "journaled" a word? I don't know, but as long as the spelling police don't read this, I'll be OK.

He said it might help to write in a journal, and I said I might have trouble thinking of things to write about. He said write what I'm feeling, what's on my mind, what's bothering me. And that it might help to imagine that I'm talking to someone I really really trust. Telling them things I want them to know. So, though I know you'll never read this... this is for you, Dad.

Soooo... what can I say about my first session? Oh, yeah. When Aunt Kathy told me about him, she said he was a Christian counselor. I just didn't get that vibe from him, though. He's a very nice man. You could even say he's... grandfatherly. Hehe. But the last time I went to church was when Sarah was nearly thrown out for being pregnant and not married. It's all good for them to preach what they want to preach, but if they can't follow it, then I don't see the point. I seem to recall Jesus talking about love... it's kind of hazy, though. I do not want to be associated with those people, and it's not just because of how they treated my sister. That was the last straw, but they were shallow and judgmental long before that. Hypocritical too. Like when old Mrs. Barr made a fuss about my skirt being too short, yet I've seen a 40 year-old photo of her wearing a sun dress of about the same length. I could tolerate stuff like that, but... they wanted to throw Sarah out! Throw her out of a supposed house of God! That left a horrible taste in my mouth. The others have gone back, to different churches, but I haven't. So, anywho, I expected a "Christian counselor" to be a lot more pushy about religion. To tell me that I'm a sinner and going to Hell and whatnot. That's the stuff Christians like to say, right? Well, maybe I'm generalizing. But I didn't expect to want a second visit. I really just went so I could tell Aunt Kathy I did. But I enjoyed talking to him. I did. We just kind of talked. I had kind of expected a lecture. Well, I guess I'd say the little girl in me expected a lecture. The rest of me didn't know what to expect. I hadn't ever been to any kind of counselor or

White Friday

therapist before. But he was nice. We talked. He's a good listener, which I guess makes sense for a counselor. Toward the end, he asked me if I have a relationship with God. I said "I guess not." I pray now and then, yeah, but only as a last resort, really. And I don't expect it to work. He was okay with it, though. What he said was... let me make sure I get it right... he said he'd like me to consider a relationship with God, but it has to be my decision. And if I felt like opening up a Bible and reading some Psalms or the Gospels, that'd be fine too. That was the extent of the God talk. So I kind of wonder if he's like, a half-hearted Christian or something? I don't know. I just thought it was weird. But I feel better after talking with him, so I agreed to do it again. Mom and Aunt Kathy are paying, so, why not? I can't tell Kyle, though. That kind of stinks, but I can see their point. He does kind of get mad when I do things like this. Without him. I can see him flipping out. That's part of the reason why I'm telling this stuff to you, Dad. You're tougher than him. You were, at least. I like to think that you still are :)

June 13
I'm sorry I haven't written in here for a

couple days. Also I hate to say it, but I'm only writing in here now because I need to. I'm just down today. I feel like... I feel like I'm doomed. I feel like I'm never going to do anything worthwhile, and Kyle's going to leave me, and I'll be alone for good and I'll have to move back in with mom or something... I want to cry, but I can't. I tried telling Kyle how I feel. I DID tell him how I feel. Then he said I might feel better if we went to the buffet for dinner. That was his entire response. I asked if he heard what I said. And he said "What do you want me to do?" And I couldn't answer him because I really didn't know. That was a horrible feeling too. I tried to sit down and watch TV with him... I just couldn't, though. I couldn't stand it. So now I'm locked in the bathroom writing this. And he hasn't knocked on the door to see how I am. I kind of wish he would, even though I'd tell him to go away.

I don't hear the TV anymore. Or anything else. I wonder what he's doing.

June 14

So things got a little bit better last night. Kyle went out and got us Chinese food, including egg drop soup, which is wonderful.

White Friday

As soon as he saw me, he hugged me. Food and hugs always work :)

I don't know what was going on with me. I feel a little bit better today, but not entirely. I actually feel kind of numb. When we went to bed, he wanted to do it. You know. I didn't want to, but I let him. It's easier than saying no and dealing with his tantrum.

Feels like my talk with Dr. Bethune was like a month ago... it's only been a few days. I'm looking forward to Monday.

June 15

I've been thinking about the Bible thing. No harm in reading some. I did go to Sunday School, after all, and I turned out okay. Kyle has his mom's old Bible, so I got it out. He asked what made me want to read that. I said I just felt like reading something old and historical.

"Lord, how are they increased that trouble me! Many are they that rise up against me." Boy, I've been feeling like that. I know there's no one "rising up against me," really, but I still feel like that. The Bible makes a lot of bold claims, though, I will say that.

I cried a little today. No real reason.

June 17

Okay, so Dr Bethune asked me to write about what makes me the most happy and what makes me the most sad. Well. My wedding was definitely one of the happiest days of my life. I believe Kyle would say the same thing... I had always pictured having rice thrown at me after my wedding, but I think the bubbles turned out to be a lot more fun. Also we saved a few of those bubble things for the honeymoon :)

What else? Spending time with mom, of course. Seeing Sarah... but visiting Billy just makes me sad. I love him, of course, but what he did was inexcusable and now he's paying for it. I guess I really like nature... I'm no tree-hugger, but outside is usually a real nice place to be. I like to hike or just explore... Wheeler Park, Coleman, Crockett, places like that. McFarland, of course, I almost took that place for granted because I'm so used to it. Natchez Trace, we had some fun there... Also books. I guess I have simple pleasures, huh? I saw <u>Watership Down</u> at the used bookstore and I was so curious about it because it seemed like EVERYONE read it in high school except me. So unfair. So I got it and, wow... beautiful.

White Friday

And thrilling. And tragic, but mostly in a "circle of life" kind of way. Surprisingly effective for a story about bunnies. I started out with dad's old Stephen King collection, when I was 14... but I'll read anything. Food, of course. I mean, I don't overeat, but... I'm so glad I was born in Bama :) That includes cooking. If I get to watch others enjoy something, that makes me just as happy as enjoying it myself. That reminds me, I need to get that pot pie recipe from mom... it's like, her signature dish. I want to make it for Kyle.

The worst time of my life was when dad died. Yes, Dad, I know you couldn't help it, but when you went, I just couldn't deal with it. I'm so glad to still have mom, but you were my favorite person. Yes. The times we all spent at the Fair were just... perfect. And the days you took us fishing were pretty wonderful too. I may be wrong, but I always felt like you and I had a special... bond, or something. Like when Sarah and Billy were doing their teenage things, and I, being the baby of the family, didn't have any friends around, you became my friend. That's what made you so important to me, and of course that's why it hurt me so much when you were suddenly gone. It's kind of funny... and sad... how the thing that makes you happiest can become the thing that makes you saddest. It's kind of wrong. Definitely unfair. But some things just work that way, I guess.

The other stuff is kind of common sense. When people are rude to me or disappoint me... I'm sad. Billy's situation makes me sad. I'm kind of sad that I haven't been able to go to college... but my reading helps. Occasionally I worry about Kyle at work, even though he can handle himself. Bad things can still happen... like what happened to you, dad...

Sometimes I just feel sad and I don't know why. Not just around my period, either. Some nights I can't sleep, and I lie awake staring into the darkness, listening to Kyle snoring away and letting frightening thoughts run through my head.

June 20

I was rereading some Harry Potter last night, just because they're fun and easy to read... well... Kyle pulled the book out of my hands. He said "Why do you have to read all this fluff?" I was speechless. He never said anything about my reading before. Then he said it worries him, how I'm constantly "retreating" into made-up stories. He's afraid that I can't deal with the real world. He says I should at least be reading "real" stories, non-fiction, I guess he meant. Maybe he's right. He is a lot more "street smart," I guess you could say. I suppose I could stand to be more like him. I hope it's not a waste of time to read fiction, though.

June 21

I was reading, same book as the other day, Kyle walks in and grabs it from me, again. He says he thought I would have learned from our previous discussion. Then he throws it in the garbage, the kitchen garbage. He said it was for my own good. I wanted to get it out, but it had tuna juice and other stuff on it and just... augh. I tried to yell, but I was so upset I couldn't get very loud. He said he's trying to make me into a better, stronger person. Someone who doesn't need fairy tales to get through life. I said he never asked me to stop reading them. He said it was implied. I didn't know what to say after that. I stormed off to the bedroom. He came in a minute or two later and wanted me to forgive him. He kept saying he was doing it for me, he wanted to improve me... Of course, this isn't the first time he has started a fight and then come back all sorry when I walked away. He's got some temper on him. I don't know where it comes from.

One minute, he's the sweetest guy ever, then, boom, crazy with anger or jealousy or something. I guess maybe I'll ask him to recommend some books for me to read.

August 2

Kyle is out muddin' with Frank and a couple other guys... hopefully he comes home in a good mood. I took mom out for lunch and some shopping. Her knees are getting pretty bad. She may need a wheelchair or one of those scooters pretty soon. I almost can't bear to watch her deteriorate like this, considering what a pillar of strength she was during most of my childhood. I mean, parents are the people you look up to so much when you're young, you think they can do anything, fix anything... They're kind of like the real-life versions of super heroes. Then they start to slowly lose their powers. It's horrible. Cause if it can happen to them, it can happen to anyone. Plus my siblings aren't around to share the burden. She doesn't talk about them much, but I'm sure they cross her mind. Thank God Aunt Kathy comes over from Athens a couple times a month. Oh, you might not believe it, dad, but Uncle Bill's auto shop is actually doing well enough to expand! I was little, but I remember you sayin' he was getting in over his head.

    And... I guess I should write about this. I've been trying not to think about it, but it's become more and more obvious over the past month or so. There was the test, but I didn't trust it. I went to see a doctor while Kyle was at work yesterday and it turns out there is a baby inside me. They didn't call it a baby, of course, but using the word "fetus" just seems so cold. Baby was conceived about six weeks ago... I think I remember the night. This is... frightening. I know I can do it, but things are going to change. My body is going to change. Little baby... big impact. I hope Kyle doesn't feel pressured to provide more, he gets enough stress from work as it is. Or at least he says it's from work. Hopefully they decide about that supervisor position soon... he really deserves it. We could use the extra money regardless... but with the baby, we will probably <u>need</u> it.

    How am I going to tell him? And when? It's a big thing to bring up. I haven't even been sick that much. Maybe I'm overthinking it, though. We both want to be parents... some day. We haven't been specifically trying for it... but I guess "some day" is going to be sooner than we thought. So, of course this is a good thing. But why am I scared to tell him? Am I... unbalanced? Nah. I just need to find the right moment. Yes, he is hot-tempered, but we are crazy about each other :)

August 3

He was out so late that I had gotten bored and turned on the TV. Fortunately I've been remembering to hide my books when I'm not reading them. It was after ten when I heard his truck outside. Apparently some friend of a friend named Roger had gone along at the last minute and of course he ended up with a broken collarbone. I tell ya, the rookies always get hurt when these guys go out to play. Rite of passage, maybe. Anyway, Kyle was caked with mud all over... he seemed to like it, too, like a little boy. I told him to take off everything dirty before coming in... he said he couldn't take off his mind. Haha. He ended up coming in with nothing but his boxers and his boots. Of course they left mud clumps everywhere he walked. I told him he would have to clean that up. He said "Uh-uh!" and pushed me into the bedroom. Now I suppose it's some kind of redneck fetish to make love with nothing but your boots on, but I just wasn't feeling it. I still feel weird and I'm getting used to thinking that there's a baby in me and, well, I slapped his hand away. I just didn't think I could do it right then. But then he slapped me and I realized I could.

August 4

Wow. I feel like I got a lot of... stuff... out of me today. I had to, I needed to tell someone. Thank God for Dr Bethune. He hardly even asked any questions this week, maybe he should get paid less for that session. Ha ha. This was the first time I've seen him look disturbed, though. I mean, there are different things that I don't tell different people, but I told it ALL to him. Maybe told him too much. But I had to. I couldn't go home, either. Kyle's not home yet, of course, but I just felt like riding the bus to McFarland Park. That's where I am now. Just lookin' out at the river and thinkin'. Maybe things will be okay. Dr Bethune was encouraging. He said that me telling him all that was a big step, and he was proud that I did it without any prodding. Maybe I can even get Kyle to come with me one of these days and we'll get our problems sorted out for good. But first I have to tell him about our baby.

August 7

I don't know if I can write it. No, I guess I can. I've stayed in bed the past couple days. I feel like such a lump. I couldn't bear to show my face outside. I've been telling Kyle I'm sick. He probably doesn't believe me, but, well, that doesn't change much, does it? He didn't get the supervisor position, I don't know why. Apparently they brought in someone from another store to oversee them. It's very disappointing. For me. It's worse for Kyle. So one of his buddies at the store took him out for a couple drinks after work. But he didn't get out all of his anger before coming home. God, I hope he never finds this. I guess he was being passionate or whatever, but he smacked my head pretty hard against the wall when he kissed me. And then the bedroom... God help me... it was bad. I guess I can repair those jeans sometime when I get bored and need a project. I looked in the mirror the next day and saw what looked like an abuse victim from Law and Order, only it was me. Not some gorgeous actress wearing black and blue makeup. I wanted to stop him, I tried, but I couldn't without hurting him. And I couldn't hurt him... Sex used to be good for

White Friday

both of us, now it's only good for him.
What happened?

August 8

I called Aunt Kathy. I couldn't tell mom. I suppose I'll have to sooner or later. Uncle Bill is coming to get me now. I packed a few things.

9

Craig stepped out of apartment 116 with his head in his hands. He wanted to say "Wow," but all that came out was "Ughhh."

"Too much information?" Cheryl was standing in the doorway.

"A little," said Craig. "It doesn't change my opinion, but... ughh... your poor turtle..."

"I should've seen it coming," said Cheryl. Clearly she had come to terms with it.

Craig braced himself against the opposite wall. "You did the only thing you could—getting the hell out of there."

Cheryl just nodded, her eyes wide in a 'you have no idea' expression.

"One thing I don't understand... from what I've heard, you guys both have awesome families. Why aren't you with them?"

A cheer of "YES! GO! GO!" erupted from the apartment. Sid had just risen from the couch as a team in black scored a touchdown on the TV. Cheryl glanced back at him and smiled to herself. Then she held up her left hand... there was a wedding band on her ring finger.

Craig habitually looked for rings on the hands of most women he met—but Cheryl and Sid had been together since he met them. She was taken, so there had never been any point in examining her hands. His heart leapt into his throat. It was a typical wedding band, nothing special... but he knew of no better couple on campus. This was... awesome.

"This is what you call a grad student honeymoon," said Cheryl, with no trace of bitterness or remorse.

"But—when?"

"Tuesday, after we got out of class." She smiled, looking perfectly content.

Then it occurred to Craig that two of his good friends had been married for three days and he hadn't heard a peep out of them. "Hey... I thought we were friends! I didn't see anything about this... you know, online or anything..."

"We, uh... haven't told our families yet." She seemed slightly less content with this... but not unhappy.

"Ooh," said Craig, wincing. No matter how awesome their families were, he knew they wouldn't be happy to hear that they had missed the ceremony.

"I know," she said, as if hearing his thoughts. "But... as you're fond of saying, Craig, now is the time."

"It is," he said. "It certainly is." He clasped her hands in his. "Congratulations to both of you. I hope you survive Christmas."

Glenn stood at the front door of the building, looking out. This afternoon seemed to have lasted for days rather than hours. And the sun still had not set.

He had received a text message as they left Ashley's suite—a message from her phone, in fact. **I'm playing in**

the snow!!! it read. This had struck Glenn like an arrow in his lung, for reasons that he did not want to acknowledge at the moment. He had escorted Eric back—to his and Craig's suite, of course—as calmly as possible. Then Glenn had slipped away and hurried down the two flights of stairs to see who, exactly, was playing in the snow with Ashley's phone.

The untouched snow almost seemed to glow, reflecting what little light could escape the clouds. The original snow angel remained, though its outline had been dulled by the continuous snowfall. Someone had made another angel a couple feet away, sharp and recent. Very recent—the author of that new angel had tracked snow into the lobby, and it had just begun to melt. This person had apparently taken off their shoes and brushed off excess snow before returning to their room—no tracks to follow.

How fitting. He had nothing... no clues to follow and no idea what might have become of Ashley's body. The trespassing in her suite with Eric had been interesting, but not helpful. It seemed that she had drank a lot of water recently... but what, if anything, could that mean? Water bottles laying around... there had been one in the laundry room, too. Why not just refill her sport bottle and drink from it? The water pitcher had been sitting out, empty. And there had been a handwritten note on the refrigerator, which Eric had apparently not noticed: **new water filter**. Glenn and Craig also kept bottled water in their fridge because the tap water on campus was, well... not great. One of those filter pitchers seemed expensive compared to a case of bottled water, but it probably would have paid for itself in the long run, considering that utilities like water were included in the rent. Oh well.

Eric seemed to have lost interest in the search for Ashley. He had simply sat down on the couch and stared at his laptop, looking preoccupied. Something about

Sam's room had apparently affected him; Glenn was not great at reading people, but he could tell that at least. Well, he had gotten what he could out of his uninvited guest, and now Eric would probably rush to soothe his reopened wounds with booze, or pills... or both. No great loss.

Eric opened his refrigerator and took out a beer. He cast a disappointed glance toward the three remaining bottles; he'd bought twelve on Tuesday. Sasha was the only other person around for the weekend who had alcohol, and he didn't want to see her for a while.

She had... well... she had not betrayed him. But she had gone too far. She had taken threads of what might become love, woven them into a tapestry of hate, and tried to present it to him as a gift. Like a loyal dog laying a mangled bird at its master's feet. The owner does not appreciate the gift, and the dog does not understand why. Then, perhaps, the owner begins to realize that he and his canine companion are vastly different creatures, who will never see the world in quite the same way. Eric had come to the same realization about his current girlfriend.

He had always known there was something off about her. All it took was to see her wandering the building in nothing but a towel, considering they all had showers inside their apartments. Sex, however, has a way of creating its own truths. They seem as bright and solid as day while flesh is rubbing against flesh... but as personalities begin to clash, they become foggy and shapeless. Then one sees that they are not really truths at all, only sensations. But then... how were they any different from what those colorful pills made him feel? The ones sitting on the counter in front of him?

He didn't know. Or, at the very least, he couldn't say.

He picked up the bag... felt the weight of the pills,

fifteen or so... and stuffed it in his hip pocket. He needed them... on his person, at least. He would go back to Glenn and Craig's place... partially because he had left his stuff there... and partially because he had come to the conclusion that a roommate was a good thing to have. So far, he had spent his college career living in a single apartment—perhaps because he had become so comfortable spending evenings alone in his room back home. Here at school, he had always been socially—and romantically—active enough to avoid significant loneliness. Then he dated Sam. He had spent a lot of time at her place. And he had never seen a pair of roommates who got along as well as Ashley and Sam. They reminded him of a pair of sisters he had known—and dated—in high school. These sisters had been two years apart, and had naturally hung out in different crowds... but they never missed family time nor took it for granted, and each sister knew she could lean on the other whenever needed. He had marveled at the way Sam and Ashley cooked, cleaned, and, despite their different majors, studied together. And even if they didn't interact... if Ashley simply passed through while Eric and Sam were cuddling on the couch... it made a difference. Life was nearby. He would feel increasingly isolated whenever he went back to his apartment, which felt so perfunctory compared to a suite. A shoebox next to a mansion. Then he had been... evicted... from Sam's place. Sasha had come along about a week later, and she had welcomed him, most of the time, into her suite. He had remarked on the overflowing garbage can in the kitchen and the unruly piles of DVDs and CDs in the living room: "Doesn't your roommate mind?"

"My roommate chickened out," Sasha had replied. "Ran away to her ogre of a boyfriend."

"Why?"

"Because she's a major league cunt," Sasha had said,

much too casually. Eric had not brought up the subject again. And now he was beginning to understand why someone would move out of their assigned apartment, away from their assigned roommate, in the middle of a semester. There was something sad about Sasha, still. She knew she had been abandoned... but she couldn't seem to understand why. So, she pretended everything was okay. But Eric had observed her chronic insomnia. He had heard the crying when she locked herself in the bathroom, at least once a week. He didn't feel like slapping and choking her during sex as she demanded, at least not all the time... and he was increasingly frustrated by the regular occasions on which she did not want to be touched at all. The roommate drama had not caused these things. The roommate drama was just another symptom.

He felt close to her... after all, he had spent more nights in her bed over the past month than he had in his own. He wanted to help, but she simply refused to talk about herself in a serious manner. He had suggested a therapist; Sasha had snorted and said, "Mom's a shrink. They don't help." Finally, he had taken what he saw as a big risk, considering how his last relationship had ended, and offered Sasha some Ex. He had read somewhere on the internet that Ex had therapeutic effects on some people, so maybe it would help. Sasha accepted his offer, although she had insisted it was "just for fun." The tablet had been in her system for two minutes when she complained of nausea. Before he could stop her (as if he could have anyway), she had swallowed her three remaining Valium and shut herself in her bedroom to sleep it off.

Sasha clearly needed help, and Eric could not provide it. But he also couldn't hate her on account of her issues. He had spent much of the afternoon thinking about it. Her latest misstep was bouncing around in his head, and he was still upset about it... but in time, and assuming no one had been hurt, he might be able to forgive her. Eric believed in second chances... sometimes even third and fourth chances. Did their relationship have a shot? Perhaps not. He wanted to build a mature relationship with a stable woman. But did Sasha deserve to be forgiven for mental and emotional problems that she could not control? Absolutely.

On the way back to Glenn's apartment, Eric stopped in front of Ashley's door. He looked at the scarecrows... one male and one female.

He pulled out his phone and texted Sasha. He knew she would be waiting to hear from him, hopeful that he'd change his mind. But he texted simply, **Have you seen Ashley?**

To be perfectly honest, he would rather have seen Sam. He had a couple of important things to tell her. The first thing being that she might be in danger at the dorm. Second, that he was willing to do whatever necessary to win her back.

Excerpts from Ashley's Journal

October 25

Uncle Bill took his friend Gary and went over to Florence. I saw them stashing some guns in the truck. They came back about 5 hours later with Kyle's signature on the divorce papers... though they were slightly crumpled. I couldn't sit still while they were gone. I could hardly think. I have so many questions I'd like to ask Uncle Bill, but I can't right now. I just... can't deal with people right now.

Should I be relieved? Should I be happy? Should I be crying? I don't know. I don't think I feel anything. It's confusing. I thought that if my marriage was officially over, I'd be a wreck. Maybe there's something wrong with me. I wonder what Kyle is feeling now. What he's doing. Who he's with.

Anyway, it is over. It is over. What do I do now? Now my life seems like a great wide open and I have no idea what to fill it with. Other than being a mom, of course. I don't care what anyone says, I have been taking care of this child since before I even knew it was there. I have been a mother for 4 months now. And that's part of the reason why Uncle Bill decided to go and force the issue with Kyle. I should be free of him and focused on making a good life for me and my baby, at least that's what they said. I kind of agree, but, I don't know where to begin.

I can hear my aunt and uncle talking out in the kitchen, but I'm just not ready to go out there.

October 26

Kyle was here late last night, banging on doors, throwing rocks, hollering. Uncle Bill told me to stay in my room, then he took his shotgun and went to the door. He was there for around 5 minutes. There was some shouting, but I couldn't make out what they were saying. I imagine Kyle feels like he's been defeated, but he won't let it go without having the last word. That kind of thing was attractive when we were dating... it's just kind of scary now. I don't know how far he'll go. Last night he broke a window and damaged some of the siding. And it's my fault. It's because I'm here. They say it's nice having a young person in the house again while Kristen is away at college. But they can't be on guard, looking out for me every minute of every day, and I'm afraid that's what they'll have to do with me around. I feel like I've gotten myself into something I'll never get out of.

October 29

I get to be the office assistant at Uncle Bill's auto shop, which is nice. I needed something to do. And they're busier than I imagined. And I think just about every male employee in the place has come around asking who the cute new office girl is :)

October 30

I talked to Dr Bethune on the phone for a while. He said a lot of things, mostly good. Like, for example, turning the other cheek is one thing, but husbands and wives are supposed to love and support one another. And yes, Christians believe in forgiveness, but just cause you forgive someone doesn't mean you have to keep putting up with what they're doing to you. Also he suggested I write down my goals—the vital, important ones—and find a way to make them happen. So, here goes.

<u>Goals</u>
-Provide a safe environment for my child.
-Get a stable job.
-Get some kind of education so I can improve my circumstances.

White Friday

Stacey at the shop thinks I should try to reconcile with Kyle, for the sake of the baby. He or she shouldn't have to grow up with just one parent, she says. I spent too much time, though, and too much energy getting over him. August and September... days and nights of misery. I never want to go through that again. I'm not going back.

November 2

Oh God, it's never going to end. He was there when we left work. Just leaning on his truck and watching us. I'm so glad I ride with Uncle Bill. He's been my guardian angel these past few months. I'll never be able to thank him enough. I think the best thing I can do for him is to go. Go away. Where, how, when, I don't know, but I've been a burden, and they deserve some relief. He's going to try and get us a restraining order, which sounds good, but I think I'll be better off when Kyle has no idea where I am. He doesn't deal with a bruised ego very well.

November 4

Okay, we've talked about things. Things regarding me and my baby and my future.

Uncle Bill is going to contact his brother. Who lives in Maryland. Who he hasn't spoken to in 4 years, since their mother died. It's a little bit embarrassing. I wish I didn't have to be the cause of all this fuss. But if the two brothers end up on speaking terms again, I might take credit for that...

November 5

Annnnnd they're talking! Uncle Bill and Uncle Hank! Aunt Kathy took me in the kitchen and hugged me and we jumped up and down like little girls. Apparently Uncle Bill has always been upset about how things ended between him and his brother. I guess I get the credit for bringing them back together... or at least providing a good excuse :)

I guess Uncle Hank and Aunt Carol are empty-nesters too. Maybe they'll let me stay with them for a while.

November 7

Okay, so, we're driving up to Cumberland this weekend to see Uncle Hank and Aunt Carol. They haven't seen me in... almost a decade. It's weird, Uncle Bill and Aunt Kathy have been almost like parents to me over the past few months, and now we're going on a family trip. Haha. I'm excited and, yes, kind of nervous. I think this might be, like, an audition, to see if they like me enough to let me stay with them.

November 10

Maryland is colder than what I'm used to. But otherwise it's nice. They showed us around a little, and everything went well, I think. Uncle Bill and his brother seemed like old pals. Good seafood here. If I get to stay here, I'll have to check out Baltimore... Inner Harbor and all that.

November 12

Wow. Okay. Um. Uncle Hank and Aunt Carol have agreed to let me stay with them. Indefinitely. They have one requirement: that I go to college. I talked to them on the phone tonight, they seem really happy to help, mostly because we're family. They'll help me with the baby, too. I promised that I'd pay them back for everything once I'm through school and all. They said they'll accept that. The way they see it, I deserve a helping hand because my family kind of fell apart after dad died. I definitely agree with that second part. And as far as the "helping hand" is concerned, I'll make sure they don't regret it.

This is a lot to process. Not entirely in a

bad way. I could be a college student this time next year! And I hardly have any possessions to my name right now. Haha. That's kind of sad and... liberating at the same time. But I do have family.

Sasha laid down the journal. She needed a break. She had always just assumed that Ashley's pre-Tomlin life had been one of quaint country contentment. A stern but loving father who came home sweaty after working with his hands all day long. A prudish mother who was constantly cookin' and cleanin' and bein' sexually available for her man. Perhaps five or six siblings, most of them rambunctious, all of them lovable in that confident but uncomplicated Southern way. And they would all come together for a big dinner every night—one of those families that made lots of noise regardless of the mood. Perhaps they had even owned a farm... yes, that would have fit perfectly. But the journal told an unexpected story: Ashley had had a real life. Just like she, Sasha, had had. Real life meant fear, disappointment, discouragement. Parents who didn't nurture. Siblings who didn't help. Ashley had not experienced the exact things Sasha had, but they had both lived real lives. Frighteningly real. Ashley had been through so much; Sasha had never expected that. The story had actually begun to affect her. If she kept reading, she'd probably start to cry... and when *that* seal broke, the tears could flow for hours.

So, she put down the journal, unfolded her long legs, slowly stood and stretched. She bumped up the thermostat one degree as she passed it; she was in her underwear again and it felt as if the cold from outside had started to seep in. In her room, she opened the bottom desk drawer, poured three fingers of brandy into a tumbler and took a blue and white capsule from an unlabeled orange prescription bottle. Of course, she knew those pills by sight, and had for years. *Blue and white makes you feel right.* She swallowed a mouthful of brandy, popped the pill into her mouth, followed by more brandy. It went down about as smoothly as one would expect. And she would start feeling right... right soon.

And... a phone was ringing—a grating series of insistent beeps, what she imagined an important person's phone must sound like. This was not the outdated model sitting with her clothes out in the dining area; this was her own phone. Sleek, slim, swathed in pink, and sitting on her desk. She grabbed it and looked at the screen. The name of the caller was 'Winter home.' She pressed the talk button and pressed it against her ear. "Hellooo!"

"Hello, dear," said Madeline Goldsmith. "Have you enjoyed your Thanksgiving break so far?"

"Oh so much."

"I'm glad to hear it. Did you shop at all today?"

"No, no. It's been snowing like a bitch here for like twenty-four hours, mother."

"I know I didn't teach you to speak like that..."

"You didn't teach me anything worth a fuck, did you?"

"Please, listen, dear. According to the bank, you've been overdrawn for almost a week now, and I—"

"Well you didn't teach me to be responsible with money, either!"

A pause. "Apparently not."

"So, put some more money in."

Another pause. "I suppose that if I don't, your father will."

"Well yeah, he does love me, after all."

Yet another pause. "Dear, I hope that you receive a

lesson on the meaning of real love, sometime in the near future."

Sasha chuckled. "As if I need it. Is Daddy around?"

She heard Madeline Goldsmith sigh, then the sounds of the phone changing hands.

"Hello, sweetheart." It was a strong, smooth voice. It was him.

"Daaa-deee!"

"What's happening?"

"I 'unno..."

"You dunno?"

Her lips spread into a wide smile; she cocked her head. "I 'unno."

"I think you do, babe," said Daddy.

She giggled. "I guess I was just resting. I got sweaty a little while ago..."

"With anyone important?"

"Maybe..."

"You love to make me jealous, don't you?"

"I don't knowwww," she practically sang. "I can't help it that there are boys here. And you hardly ever visit..."

"One of the next two weekends, babe, I swear."

"No mom."

He chuckled. "Of course no mom."

After finally hanging up and swallowing the rest of her brandy, Sasha looked at her phone again. She had received a text message from... Eric. Wonderful. She kicked the nearby wall. Now that she had connected with Glenn, the breakup process with Eric would have to begin. Maybe.

She opened the message. **Have you seen Ashley?**

Oh. Shit. People were looking for Ashley now? Why couldn't they just relax and enjoy their holiday weekend? She stood there for a minute, shifting her weight from leg to leg, looking around, thinking. Her gaze drifted toward the hall, then the kitchen...

The kitchen.

She strode into the small kitchen and opened the refrigerator, sticking her head in as far as she could. Yes... the shelves *could* come out.

She went back to her room, grabbed her laundry basket and, without thinking, tried to lift. Too heavy. She would have to drag it.

10

Glenn sat at his dining table, hands clasped in front of him, watching Little Craig do nothing. He had searched all three of the stairwells, from the ground floor to the locked hatches that led to the roof. He had searched the gym and the lounge, the only other common rooms currently open to the residents. He could not think of anywhere else to look. Ashley was gone and it was his fault.

A toilet flushed... *his* toilet... and out from the bathroom came Eric. Staring intently at the area two inches ahead of his eyes, he seemed caught up in his own little world. He sat down in the middle of the couch, took a swig of beer, and went back to working half-heartedly on his laptop.

Glenn shot him a glare that went unnoticed. He didn't care how lonely or contemplative Eric might be; this squatting was just rude, and he shouldn't have allowed it to start, let alone to continue. His eyes fastened themselves onto Eric's delicate, rosy-cheeked face. *Poor you. You don't work, that I know of, so someone else is paying your bills. You spend your nights and weekends drunk or stoned or whatever the hell it is you do. You're dating a gorgeous young woman who loves sex so much that she'll seduce random guys to get it. What, did you two have a fight over the last joint? Or maybe you couldn't agree on a sexual position? Yeah, life is tough. That certainly gives you the right to invite yourself into an acquaintance's apartment and sulk. You don't have any problems. Who have you lost, you girly-faced coward?!*

Finally, Glenn spoke up: "So, you and Sasha, you're fighting?"

Eric glanced at him and grunted.

Even those who didn't know Eric well knew that his relationships never lasted more than a couple months. And he didn't exclusively date loose, unstable women, as far as Glenn could tell. There had been Sam, after all. The common denominator in all of those failures: Eric. "What did you do?"

Eric did not react; he simply pretended that he'd stumbled upon the most interesting web site in the world.

Glenn stood up. He didn't know why exactly, he just felt that a man should be standing when saying something like this: "You know, your conquests would be more impressive if you actually managed to hold onto them for more than a couple months."

Eric turned and flung his beer bottle in the same motion; had Glenn still been seated, it would have smashed into his head. Instead it bounced off the wall onto the floor, clanging all the way. Both men had frozen, Glenn staring at his uninvited guest, whose eyes were locked on the bottle as it continued to roll across the tile floor of the dining area. Glenn was a bit startled, but not surprised. That was the kind of reaction he had been shooting for.

"I totally thought that would break," said Eric.

White Friday

Can't even muster the strength to break glass. "Get out," Glenn said. Forceful, but not loud.

Eric grabbed the remote, put up his feet on the coffee table, and turned on the TV.

Glenn stared at him, indignant. He couldn't believe this, and yet... he could. It actually explained a lot. He glanced at the TV; John Wayne and that other guy were still... searching.

Three taps, barely audible, at the door of the suite. It almost sounded as if someone were trying to determine whether the door was solid or hollow. But Glenn heard it, and he stepped quickly toward the door. Through the peephole he saw... Craig's nose, and then the rest of him. Glenn glanced back at his extremely unwelcome guest—Eric's attention appeared to be fixed on the TV. So, Glenn quietly opened the door, just far enough to accommodate him, and slipped out. The door shut itself, as always.

Craig's brow was furrowed and he looked slightly contrite. "Any luck?"

Glenn shook his head, opened his mouth to speak... then reconsidered. Eric was still nearby. It may have seemed slightly paranoid, but then, this was perhaps the most serious situation he'd ever been in. There could, in fact, be a murderer living among them. He grabbed Craig's shoulder and pushed him toward the center stairwell. Craig went along easily.

His roommate leaned against the railing on the stairwell landing and looked straight at him. Glenn had seen this look before, and it heartened him; Craig was in *you can trust me* mode. "Glenn," he said calmly, "what exactly happened?"

Glenn's mouth was dry. "Uhm... exactly..." he stammered. It felt as if he had writer's block, only the block was holding back reality instead of fiction. As if a dam had been built between his brain and his mouth. There was one particular word he did not want to say...

but, what else was there? The spiraling structure of this afternoon had been built upon a single stark, sobering truth. That was all he could say; that was all there was. "Ashley is... dead."

Craig stared at him for about thirty seconds, maintaining eye contact as if some vital information were being transferred within their gaze. Perhaps he was expecting a follow-up remark, some clarification, some kind of "in a manner of speaking" qualification. There was none. That fact solidified more and more over every second they held eye contact. Finally Craig's gaze drifted off toward the wall. He exhaled loudly. He raised his hands as if to make some gesture, then simply gave up.

Glenn understood. Words were pointless. Gestures were pointless. One could only... absorb reality.

Finally Craig let out a shout that sounded like a deflating balloon.

Glenn felt as though he had just found her, lying motionless on the floor of the elevator. Looking like an Ashley suit, vacated and tossed aside. Then he was carrying her, through unending hallways and feeling no body heat whatsoever. Then he went backward, to Thursday, Thanksgiving Day, and the—no. He would not allow himself to go there. Not yet. But sharing this truth with his roommate made him feel like he was experiencing it all again himself. Seeing Craig's face as he absorbed the news... he felt as if he had intentionally harmed his friend. But he also saw his own emotions mirrored on his roommate's face... and that made Glenn feel that maybe he wasn't completely alone here. His misery was... being shared.

Craig looked at him with an anguish that he was probably displaying as well. Then, something happened.

"Fuck this," said Craig.

"Huh?"

"Fuck it. Fuck it up its stupid ass."

White Friday

"Oh."

"Hey. I'm sorry I didn't... completely listen to you. Earlier. I was... in a different place."

Glenn just stared at him. He couldn't argue with that assessment.

Craig met his gaze for a few seconds, then a smile developed, not on his mouth, but in his eyes. "Okay. Yeah. My mind was still with Sasha. And her amazing—" He cut himself off. "Never mind."

Glenn forced a smile and nodded. He thought about how it felt to kiss Sasha... and he realized that he wanted to do it again. In fact, he wanted to wrap himself around that long, thin frame... and have all of her.

"I'm sorry, I got distracted... collateral damage, maybe... but you were right." He paused and opened his eyes wide. "You hear this? I'm saying that you're right."

Glenn nodded. For once, he didn't care about being right.

"So, tell me what you know. If someone is responsible... they'll regret being born."

Glenn hesitated, mentally shrinking back a bit from Craig's understated anger. Revenge had not been his motivation; he simply wanted to safely retrieve Ashley's body, because, God knew, she deserved some respect. Then he could find rest and, perhaps, a little bit of comfort. Of course, there was something else that seemed appealing as well—the touch of a female... like Sasha. If she so much as looked at him again, he might just have to jump her bones. He couldn't articulate why... he just wanted, more than usual, to be close to a woman, to touch and be touched. But he did not want to hurt anyone, even if they *had* caused Ashley's death. It would only cause more suffering, and he couldn't even bear to think of it right now. "Uh... I didn't find anything in Sasha's place..." Anything relevant to Ashley, at least... "Eric and I looked in Ashley's place... she's not there, of course..."

"Anything seem out of place?"

Glenn thought. He was torn between wanting to share the burden with Craig, and wanting to keep him from going on some vengeful rampage. He couldn't see any harm, though, in telling him... "There were a bunch of water bottles laying around. Empty ones. That's... about it."

Craig must have seen something on Glenn's face—uncertainty perhaps, because he stepped toward his roommate and punched him, firmly, in the shoulder. "What does your gut tell you?"

Glenn didn't have to think. "I know I've been through Sasha's place, but... the way she's been acting is just... I dunno. I'll be surprised if she has nothing to do with it."

Craig's gaze drifted away from him. "Mmm-hmm..."

"Eric has been at our place most of the afternoon... I mean, who else is there?"

Craig cocked an eyebrow. "Well, there could be others hanging around... but I happen to agree with you."

Great. They agreed... but what could they do? Sasha apparently had Ashley's phone, but he supposed there could be, however unlikely, a reasonable explanation for that. The rest of their reasoning boiled down to 'Sasha has been acting weirder than usual,' which was subjective at best.

Glenn leaned back against the wall; his head thumped lightly on the textured surface. "I searched her place..." he said, and his voice trailed off hopelessly. What he had found may have been interesting, but not relevant. Not even the... pill bottle that was still in his pocket...

"Do it again," said Craig, sounding remarkably businesslike.

"How do we, uh, get her out of there?" Glenn asked.

Then a voice rose up behind him: "You guys have a problem with Sasha?" Eric stepped into the stairwell,

White Friday

glancing back and forth between them. He didn't look completely alert... but the sharp suspicion in his eyes seemed to compensate for that.

"Not at all," said Craig. "We love her. We're about to go tag-team her right now."

Eric simply stared at him.

Glenn resisted the urge to bring his palm against his face, and thought instead, about finding something useful to say. "We're... worried about her," he said finally.

"I'll bet you are," said Eric, his eyes aimed squarely at Craig. "She told me about how you're always staring at her, undressing her with your eyes... following her..."

"Hey now," said Craig. "Just that one time."

"Are you guys planning on stealing from her, or what? You know I won't let you."

Craig scoffed and gave Glenn an amused look. "Why would we steal? She's giving it away." He paused to let those words sink in, then he gestured toward his roommate and himself. "Just today she's had both of us inside of her."

Glenn fidgeted. He didn't like hearing lies and assumptions repeated, especially in such a confident and manipulative way. It was partially his fault, though, for not being completely honest with his roommate.

Eric was simply shaking his head, watching Craig with angry eyes.

Craig went on: "You know she's not dating you because you're Eric, right? She's dating you because you have a penis!" He looked toward Glenn and chuckled as if sharing a private joke. He went on, with a smile on his face and a laugh in his voice: "Glenn wasn't even going to do her, but she kept begging for it..." He adopted his version of a female voice: "Come on, Glenn, please... I'll let you stick whatever you want wherever you want. Please, Glenn, let me be your hand puppet!"

For a moment, it looked as if Eric was turning toward

Glenn. In reality, as a lefty, he was drawing back to throw a punch at Craig. He threw said punch, catching Craig at the very bottom of his chin. Craig had been expecting it, and while he couldn't dodge it completely, he did put himself in position to wrap his arm around Craig's neck. He took hold of Craig's momentum and elaborated upon it, swinging him around toward the stairs, shoving and letting go. Glenn was certain that he glimpsed Craig's face contorted with rage as he pushed... no, *threw* Eric.

Eric tumbled. He bounced. He rolled. He came to rest on the next landing, below the sectioned picture window, and did not move any further.

Glenn watched it all, feeling totally powerless. Like one of those unpleasant but necessary scenes in your favorite movie; you can watch it again and again, hoping that it turns out differently and that everyone involved can avoid suffering... but it never works out that way. Glenn could rewind that scene and play it again, over and over, and it would go the same way every time. Eric swings at Craig. Craig throws Eric. Eric tumbles in a way that no human should. From the moment Craig swung Eric toward the steps, Glenn had wanted to do something. To leap forward and somehow catch Eric, keep him from getting hurt. And in his own mind, that had even seemed possible. But Eric had started to fall, and Glenn had not moved. Eric had continued to fall, and still Glenn had not moved. Eric had crumpled to the floor of the landing... and Glenn had stood, staring... useless. He could not have stopped any of it... and he felt like a failure. On the surface, it may have seemed simple—Glenn liked Craig and did not like Eric. But violence is ugly, even when it is necessary. And this was hardly necessary.

But Glenn had seen Craig give that enraged look before—as if every muscle in his face had been pulled taut by steel cables, strong and sharp enough to cut anyone who got close. Not often, but regularly enough that he had ceased to be surprised by it. Craig had displayed that look in September while flinging a chair across the room after a professor had rejected his twelve-page paper. It had made an appearance in October when a girl—who had flirted heavily with Craig—ended up going to the homecoming dance with a guy he hated. It had been due for an appearance here in November, Glenn supposed. Craig hardly ever showed anger, or even annoyance... but when he did, it was dangerous. It was also easy to gloss over, since he seemed so genial ninety-eight percent of the time. The question Glenn always wanted to ask, but lacked the courage to do so, was this: where did it come from? Did he save up all his anger and resentment in a deep reservoir somewhere inside? And if so... why?

Silence had filled the stairwell. Glenn felt himself perspiring, but his hands felt unpleasantly cold. He had been frozen in place ever since Eric had stepped through the door.

Craig was also still, staring down at the next landing like a tourist gazing down into a scenic gorge. He let out a long breath, slumping his shoulders and leaning against the railing. "Shit," he said.

Glenn had no words, nor did he try to find any.

"I shouldn't have done that," said Craig.

"Which part?"

Craig just shook his head, then he tensed up visibly and let out a rising cry of frustration and angst that echoed above and below.

Once the echoes had died, Craig turned, closed the distance between him and Glenn in a few steps, and grabbed his roommate by the arm.

Glenn pulled away. Good friend, roommate, yeah, but at this moment, he didn't want anyone touching him. Any male, at least. He would have welcomed a female touch, he would have pushed her against the wall and shoved his tongue down her throat...

Craig interrupted his escapist fantasy before it could escalate. "Come on. I'm sorry. I can't do this without you, though."

Glenn simply gave him a blank look. Despite appearances, he wasn't angry with his roommate. He just wasn't sure what to think. His mind was saturated with the events of the past two minutes, processing them.

Craig moved toward the down stairs. "You said the cops are coming, right? Well... we gotta find Ashley, soon. And I think we both have the same hunch."

Glenn looked at the floor. "I searched her suite," he said quietly.

"She can only access so many places," said Craig, jangling the ring of keys in his pocket. "Unlike me..."

There was a sex joke in there for the taking, Glenn knew, but he wasn't in the mood.

"I think I have an idea," said Craig hopefully. "If we can't find Ashley, maybe we can at least get Sasha to trust us... err, trust you... and maybe she'll confide in you."

Glenn raised an eyebrow. That would have to be some ingenious plan. But his roommate was right—they had to try. Ashley deserved as much.

He followed Craig down the stairs, past Eric—who appeared to be breathing—to the second floor. Once they were in the student lounge, having ensured no one was around, Craig sat on the arm of a standard dorm chair and fixed a serious gaze on Glenn. "You need to fuck her."

Glenn flinched. He had never been entirely comfortable with that phrase; it just seemed so... animalistic. "Could you stop saying that word?"

Craig looked confused for a moment. "Screw her?"

"Yes, thank you." Glenn usually didn't approach sex as simply a way to gratify oneself or blow off steam. To him, it was something special, between two people who

White Friday

wanted to be closer to each other. Also, he had been expecting a slightly more intricate plan from his roommate. "That's it?"

Craig's eyes seemed to lose focus for a moment. "You need to screw her... hard."

Glenn felt a tingling warmth spreading throughout his body. There were probably goosebumps on his arms, but he was afraid to look, afraid to move at all. Blood was flowing to his crotch, as well. He wanted to do it, he wanted to throw Sasha onto her waterbed and make waves. He wanted to explode with pleasure, and to make her explode as well. A part of him, a large part of him, wanted to erase this terrible day with rapturous sexual escapades and then collapse with pure exhaustion. But... another part of him wanted to know, *what does this have to do with Ashley?*

Craig must have noticed the nervous uncertainty on his face—he had always been good at reading people. "Just go in there and dominate her. Treat her like she's been a bad little student and you're going to punish her... with your dick."

Glenn could only stare. Was he really being asked to do this?

"Trust me," said Craig. "She'll love it. I don't know how you did it the first time, but... that's the way she likes it."

"Um... what's the point of this?"

Craig confidently raised an index finger. "Plan A, you get her into the bedroom and I will search the rest of her suite. You just have to keep her there for a while; can you do that?"

Glenn felt like an elite soldier being briefed for a dangerous mission. "Uh... yeah."

"Like, ten minutes or more?"

"Oh, yeah. I can do that standing on my head."

"She might request that position. Anyway, Plan B—" He raised a second finger— "should help if I can't find anything. Once you're finally, uh, spent... just stay there, cuddle or talk or whatever she wants to do. Don't act like her best friend, but... we want her to connect with you. Feel more than just... lust."

Glenn was okay with that. He did feel nervous, though—not about his performance—but about the fact that they had a plan. That meant something could go wrong. And, with Sasha involved, that was a good possibility. He would do it, though. He wanted it... and now he had a good excuse to do it. And best of all, he knew Sasha would be up for it. He also understood how Craig wanted him to act; basically, like an alpha male. The kind of man who would take what he wanted from a woman while convincing her that she was happy to give it. A man who, unlike Glenn, wasn't afraid to disagree with his woman, or even make fun of her at times. A man who was so comfortable in his own skin that he often made others uncomfortable in theirs. A man... very much like Craig.

They paused a moment before turning the corner toward Sasha's place. "You ready?" Craig asked. "You need any... supplies?"

Glenn thought of Sasha's desk drawers. "I'm good to go." He paused. "Are you okay? He did manage to hit you..."

Craig shrugged and looked away. There was a faint reddish spot on his jaw where part of Eric's fist had landed. "I've been hit harder."

Glenn could only nod. He had no idea to what Craig was referring.

Craig nodded back, then turned his gaze toward the stairwell; there was no sign of Eric or anyone else. "I know you're probably wondering... why," Craig said softly.

Glenn simply shook his head, then remembered that Craig was looking away. "No, man..." He never called anyone "man"... unless he was nervous.

"I want to explain anyway," said Craig. It seemed he couldn't take his eyes off the window in the stairwell door. "I don't know, it's just when people disrespect me... or give me lip... I just want to hurt them. I feel it so strongly that I just can't..." He sighed heavily. "I can keep it in most of the time. Most of the time."

"Not all of the time, though," said Glenn quietly.

Craig shook his head slowly. "I can't... I'm not... *perfect*..." His voice had the heightened quality of a pleading child trying not to cry.

"No," said Glenn to the back of his roommate's head. "You're not. Neither am I. Neither is Eric. Neither was Ashley..."

"I hope he can forgive me," said Craig, still gazing toward the stairwell. "At some point."

Glenn was momentarily lost for words. He had never seen Craig this penitent before. "Maybe... when this is over... and he knows everything..."

Craig finally looked back toward his roommate. His eyes looked weary, but there were no tears. "I'm going to make up for it by finding Ashley. I just need your help."

Glenn nodded.

"I don't mean to force you into something like this... but it's the best I can think of right now."

The plan did seem rather crude, but... they were running out of time. And besides, he was about to get laid.

Excerpts from Ashley's Journal

April 3

I've been thinking a bunch about the things Dr Bethune has told me about God. Some of the things he emphasized when I told him about my baby. We mustn't confuse Heaven and earth, he said. Heaven is a place without suffering... earth is not. The Bible says we will suffer... stuff like that. And I understand.

And the fact that God watched His own son die.

I have felt like maybe I should be angry at God. A couple of the ladies in the group are. It's really really easy, to be angry. But it doesn't make sense when I think about it. Like, say God does exist... if that's the case, then He's got to be at a higher level than us. Beyond what we can see. If He exists, then there is life beyond this existence that we know, and that would mean that when we die, it's not the end... we're just moving on somewhere else. Which means my David has moved on somewhere else. Not just... gone. To me, that takes away a lot of the pain involved with death.

If God doesn't exist... well, there's no one to be angry at, is there?

I think I believe in God.

White Friday

June 4

I think I made a friend today. His name is Craig and he lives on my floor. He was trying to look cool by lifting more weight than he could handle... Kyle used to make fun of guys who tried stuff like that. Personally, I felt kind of bad for him. He seems like a good guy. A lot of the people who normally live here are gone for the summer, so I have to make friends when I can! He seemed pretty embarrassed... I think I actually helped him deal with it. Feels good. I think that's something the group has brought out in me. Otherwise I might have minded my own business.

Of course the summer classes will keep me pretty busy for about a month. Music and Biology, two general education courses that I can't wait to get out of the way. Then, work work work until fall semester starts! I need to save up some money.

I wish David were still with me. I would welcome all the challenges of motherhood. He was only outside of me for 2 days, though he was really with me for 9 months. Motherhood isn't supposed to end like that, so suddenly. Or at all, I guess. Sometimes I still miss him enough to cry. I don't feel hopeless like I did during my marriage, though. I used to think that was just a natural female thing... but is it? I want to get to the root of these things, these feelings. That's how I chose my major. At least, I think that's what my major will be. I don't need to declare just yet.

July 15

Okay, the call center is not my ideal place to work. Let's admit that right now. But... but... I think I can do it. It's only five weeks or so. I imagine I'll just get hung up on a bunch. And while that's rude, it's something I'm willing to endure in exchange for money. Truth be told, I feel a little guilty myself for getting hired and trained and all, knowing that I'll be leaving in five weeks. But apparently this place has a high turnover rate anyway. Too bad they can't just let me work weekends during the semester. But I might need that time for schoolwork anyway. AND... maybe this sounds silly, but there's always a chance I can improve someone's day just by talkin' to them. I know most people don't like getting those calls, but maybe if I'm kind enough, caring enough... something little like that can have an effect, change someone's mood, even someone's day. That's something

White Friday

we talk about in the group :)

August 23
Well, I have already lived on campus for a little while and been through a couple of classes, but that all feels like dress rehearsal now. Tomorrow is when I actually start being a full-time student. Oh gosh. It's like, showtime. I've been over all my lists, I know I have everything I need... AND, if the summer classes were anything to go by, I'm going to pretty fine in terms of grades :)

I have met a few new people since I got back. Sam is finally here, otherwise known as Samantha, but she won't let anyone call her that. She spent her summer in New Mexico doing something with the Indians... err, Native Americans, I guess I should say. A guy named Eric came over to see her almost as soon as she arrived. He seemed nice enough.

September 5
Well here I am, watching Alabama play Virginia Tech while catchin' up on my journaling! I don't think I would have kept this up if I didn't find psychology so interesting. And also because I want to record the course of my life in some way. I sure wish I

could look back and see what I was thinking when Kyle and I were courting...

Oh, mom mailed me some money and some recipes. Can you guess which of those things made me cry? If you guessed the recipes, you'd be right. Cookies, cobbler, buttermilk fried chicken and yes, the legendary turkey pot pie. I am so blessed. Of course, a few of her recipes I had memorized already.

October 3

A couple of people to talk about. Sam is like, well... let's just say, if Sarah wanted to learn how to be a good sister, she could just watch Sam for a while. Honestly, if I could choose a sister, I would choose Sam. Luckily I get to live with her for at least this year :) I have already told her most of the significant events of my life. She has returned the favor, and, with the environment she grew up in, I'm just amazed that she's not a spoiled brat. So, her parents get a gold star for doing something right.

And Craig is kind of like an older brother. I think he might've liked me at first, but that seems to have subsided... and I think it's better that way. Glenn is an interesting creature. He can sit there quietly for an hour or more, then suddenly he'll speak up and say the perfect thing. Craig often errs on the side of saying too much. Glenn, though, will sometimes say just enough, and sometimes he'll leave me wanting more. I don't think it's deliberate... I think he's just naturally... conservative. Not in the political way. He conserves his words, conserves his energy, stuff like that. I've watched football with those two. And Glenn, 90% of the time, his biggest celebration is to make a fist and raise it to chest level. But once or twice, when something really exciting happens, I've seen him jump out of his chair and flex his muscles. Too bad he couldn't get on one of the football teams... I get the sense that if he really let loose, it'd be something to see.

October 16

It's late and I'm sleepy, but I wanted to write this down before I forget about it. I ran into Glenn as I was leaving for Cumberland. He seemed happy to see me, as usual, but he also seemed uncomfortable. When I said I was leaving for the weekend, he looked away for a few seconds, then he just said "Drive safe, Ashley." But he said it in such a serious way... it was like he really wanted to say something else. I don't know, it just seemed unnatural because he's usually relaxed around me.

Okay, sleep time. I get to see the group tomorrow!

October 24

I must say, the more I see Glenn, the more he grows on me. I mean, I liked him to begin with, at least as a friend, but... he is pretty cute. Not drop-dead gorgeous or anything, but then, none of the guys I've fallen for have been. I could get used to that face, though. And everything else seems to be in order, physically speaking. He looks out for me, holds doors, asks if I want anything when he gets up, stuff like that, which goes a long way. His sense of humor is... diverse. I mean, he laughs at crude guy stuff, usually, and he also gets intelligent humor. He's the only other person I know, under 30 at least, who enjoys the show Frasier. Of course he's smart... not in a snobby way, though. I'd almost say wise, but that word just doesn't seem right on anyone below 40. Anyway, I might have a crush on him. I'm pretty sure he has one on me, with the way he looks at me for a few seconds, smiles, then looks away. I guess that's not the firmest evidence, but... sometimes you can just tell.

White Friday

November 15

He was here. Kyle was here. He found me. He chased me up the stairs and I just kept running until I slipped at the fourth floor... I thought he was going to kill me, he was so angry... and then, Glenn was there. He must have heard the noise. It was kind of amazing what he did. I'm lucky, the halls were pretty deserted. I always thought Glenn had some kind of hidden energy or something, I don't know. But it seems he does. I'd never seen anyone stand up to Kyle, not even his own dad. Maybe that was part of his problem. Will he come back? Maybe, maybe not. I really don't know if I care anymore. I have friends here who care about me. We have campus police. Maybe I can get some mace or a taser or something. And besides all that, I'm just tired of running. I can't do it all my life... it wouldn't be much of a life if I did.

I was scared to be alone, so I slept at Glenn's place. In his bed. And he was on the floor. I had no idea they still made guys like that. Honestly, if he had wanted to make out or feel me up or something like that, I probably would have let him. That night. I mean, I think I'd like to do that stuff with him anyway, but it was really too soon. He seemed to know that. The next day, we talked, and yes, our feelings are mutual. If he really cares about me (which I think he does), he'll take it slow. I like him quite a bit, but... I just got beat up by my ex-husband. I need to ease into things. I need to feel safe. I need to trust him. I think all these things will come, of course, I just can't do it any other way.

We talked for a while. I told him about David, about the support group in Cumberland, about our goal to improve the lives of those around us... he liked that. I told him about my marriage, of course. He took it all in stride. I forgot to mention Dr. Bethune. It seems so long ago that I started seeing him.

We cuddled. It was nice. We're going to make it official, sooner or later, but there's no rush as far as I'm concerned. I've found a man who could be the one, so I want to take my time and make sure he is. We've got time. He'll be here for at least a year and a half, and I've got three and a half to go.

I almost feel better than I did before Kyle found me. Of course, my face is still sore. I'm sure his feels worse, though.

White Friday

November 26

This was the first time I didn't see any family members on Thanksgiving. Uncle Hank and Aunt Carol went to her sister's place in Roanoke. Sparta and Athens are a little far for me to drive this weekend, of course, but I'll be there over Christmas. Glenn will be in Buffalo with his parents.

We did have a good day, though. He slept a little late and missed the parade, but we got to watch football, which is just as good. Then I made THE turkey pot pie. Mom's recipe. We ate it all, it was so good. We took a very nice nap together... Then Eric and Sasha came over, with no prior warning. They did bring me a chicken, which was nice. And Sasha brought a bottle of wine, but I don't think she ever intended to open it. I don't know about Sasha, she's like, a riddle. I would love to get to the bottom of her psyche. I might be afraid of what I find there, though... Anyway, she was nice for a few minutes, then she just turned, well, bitchy. And kind of petty. I don't know what happened. But she said some terrible things, so I made an excuse for them to leave. It wasn't a great excuse, either, but they took it. Strange...

Eric was nice the whole time, though. It's a shame he had to hook up with her, after being with Sam. They both seemed pretty happy when they were together, too. Aside from the drugs. But he can do so much better than Sasha.

Well, here I am, by myself. In my head, I think it wouldn't be terrible if Glenn spent the night. But another part of me, I guess you could say my heart, keeps saying "too soon too soon too soon..." My mom used to have a charming little plaque (still does, I think) that said "the heart has its reasons, which reason cannot know." Or something to that effect. Anyway, I think we'll start spending the night together pretty soon. Keeping our clothes on, of course... that's a whole other story. I don't give myself away at the drop of a hat... but if I'd do it with anyone, it would be him. ANYwho... we'll see each other tomorrow, we'll probably play in the snow. I do hope he kisses me again like he did... it sent a tingle through me.

I've still got a sizable chunk of my Psychology book to read and summarize... it's like they punish us for having a holiday weekend by giving us extra work. Also some Algebra to figure out... I can do it, it just bores me. Numbers are so lifeless.

Sasha got me thinking about Sam's sport drink additives, so I finally decided to try one.

With Sam's water. Too lazy to refill mine right now. Hope she doesn't mind. I'll reimburse her, of course. I'm using the orange, it's always been my favorite flavor, especially in popsicles. It's pretty good, though it does have a bit of a chemical taste. I guess things that are good for you always taste a little off, the price you pay for eating and drinking healthy... sugar substitutes and things like that. I guess I should get on with my work...

Ashley drank it. Ashley drank it.

Sasha slowly slipped the journal under the covers of her bed. Ashley had drunk it, and it was her fault. And now Ashley was... well, she was... not a factor any more. Yeah, that was one way of putting it.

Ashley had been through so much. Death and despair and disappointment. Living in fear. Fleeing for safety. Letting go of the man she loved, while carrying that man's child; a constant reminder of the relationship. Carrying the child to full term, then losing him. Working shitty jobs for minimum wage, just for a chance to go to college.

Sasha crossed her arms. Reclined onto her stack of pillows. Stared up at the ceiling. It was all so unfathomable. She had known, in her head, that a lot of people lived more difficult lives than her. But through Ashley's journal, she now knew it—felt it—in her heart. There was an unpleasant warmth through her entire torso. She almost felt like she had done it all herself. She had begun to... admire Ashley.

Ashley, who had survived so many things that should have broken her heart and her spirit... and she had, seemingly, come out... better. Co-founding a support group for mothers who had lost their children. Working and fighting to get into a college. Connecting with a man who was now looking better and better to Sasha every hour. And, even more amazingly, Ashley was... the coffee.

One of Sasha's inane acquaintances had posted it online, the kind of inspirational story that people like to pass around. Sasha had skimmed it, only marginally interested... but somehow it had latched onto her brain and refused to let go. There were three kinds of people, it said—carrots, eggs and coffee. When introduced to boiling water, the carrots softened. The eggs became hardened. But the coffee... the coffee changed the water itself. Well, that had been a quaint story, a clever bit of writing, but perhaps a little too optimistic. Sasha had never known anyone who fit the description of "coffee"... until now. Ashley had often changed the environment around her... for the better. Sasha had not realized it until now. And it didn't seem to take a lot of effort, either— smiles, cookies, compliments...

And she, Sasha, had put an end to it. Her well-planned revenge had gone wrong so easily... it made her feel like an overzealous but naive child. Again. She'd thought she had life figured out and under control... but life had simply laughed and made her sorry. Again.

She had ended Ashley. And she was sorry. And frightened. And frustrated.

And... thank God for the Prozac, or else she might have felt *really* bad.

11

He knocked on Sasha's door, solidly, with confidence. He was, at the moment, an alpha male, and alpha males did not hold back out of fear of disturbing people. Everyone living in this area of the floor, had they been around, would have heard him knocking. He started to look to his right for approval from Craig, who had flattened himself against the wall on the other side of Sasha's door. Then he realized that alpha males do not need approval—in fact, they probably eschew it.

Five seconds passed, then five more. Glenn decided to eschew patience as well; he knocked again. He supposed that Alpha-Glenn should be thinking something along the lines of: *where is that miserable little bitch, and why isn't she pleasuring me yet?* Real Glenn suppressed a goofy smile at that.

The doorknob turned. The door swung inward. And there she was, in the flesh. Her wide, vibrant eyes... her juicy lips seeming to smile even in a neutral position... her skin, just so smooth and... real. He wanted to caress it. But did alpha males caress? Probably not.

When she saw it was him, her expression opened up a bit, hopeful. Glenn spoke quickly, trying to assert his will: "Hey."

She tilted her head, eyes locked on his. "I suppose you want some ass."

He looked her up and down, letting her see him do it. She was wearing only a very plush-looking robe, but purple, not pink as he would have expected. "Some..." he drawled. "I want the whole thing." In his mind, Craig was nodding with approval. The real Craig was doing no such thing.

Sasha let out a giggle, then pressed her teeth down upon her lower lip and let it slide out slowly. The effect was intoxicating.

Glenn grabbed her arm, firmly of course, and pushed his way into the suite. "Come on," he said, pulling her toward her bedroom.

Sasha let out a surprised "Oh!" but she went along without resisting. The suite looked the same as it had earlier, aside from one thing: it looked as if several bottles and jars had been taken from the refrigerator and placed on the floor in front of it—just leaving enough room to open the door. Glenn had only time to glance at it. An alarm went off in one corner of his mind, screaming "That's important!" But he had to play his role in this little charade, and Craig would certainly notice it. Besides, he was about to get laid.

But Sasha stopped him as he reached the bedroom door. Uh-oh. Something was going wrong. Perhaps they had picked the one moment in Sasha's life when she wasn't horny.

Glenn didn't look back. He simply gave her a tug and said "Come on" in an irritated voice.

Sasha giggled again, the last thing he had expected to hear. He forced a blank expression onto his face and looked back at her.

"I was about to take a shower," she said, glancing toward her adjacent bathroom. "What do you say?"

Glenn resisted the urge to cast an incriminating glance toward the front door. He hadn't expected this, but he supposed a shower would be just fine.

"You *are* dirty," he said.

A sly smile. "So are you, apparently." She tugged on the loosely tied belt of her robe and it fell open.

He had retained his grip on her arm; she backed slowly into the bathroom and he went along without resisting. She stopped near the back wall and pulled her arm free. With an exaggerated shrugging motion, she shed her robe; it fell to the floor. He looked her over, his eyes devouring every inch of bare flesh. Long and lean, and... perky. Wonderful.

Glenn took a step forward, then another, and he didn't stop until his lips were pressed against hers and her body was firmly sandwiched between his and the wall. The robe was underfoot; *let it stay there*, he thought, *for the rest of the night*. A muffled "mmm" emanated from her throat and her tongue began to wrestle with his.

This was it. This was... paradise. *Is it really this easy?*

Not with most girls.

But... why not?

You'll see.

He ignored that last thought, because he was sucking face with Sasha Goldsmith, and she was naked, and they were wrapped up in each other.

Still, it seemed too easy, didn't it?

She was pulling up his shirt. He raised his arms and allowed her to pull it off. She grinned and ran her hands down his chest. He let himself fall forward and began sucking on her neck. She giggled at first, then her arms wrapped around his back and she began to moan again. Finally she spoke up: "Are we gonna get wet, or what?"

Glenn pulled his lips from her neck and said, "You

are."

Her hands went for the front of his pants. "Mmm, you're right," she said as she worked the button and zipper. She undressed him with practiced ease.

She does have a lot of experience, after all.

Sasha put an arm around him and guided him to the side, then leaned over and reached for the shower controls. She looked up at him with those wide eyes and an intimate smile. "Socks?"

Ah. Right. Glenn leaned against the wall and hurriedly pulled off his long white socks.

This is like a hobby to her, you see.

The water was running from the spigot now. Sasha tested the temperature, then pulled up the button. The water rerouted and started spewing from the shower head almost instantly. Sasha stuck in her hand again to make sure, then stepped into the tub. She was a work of art—her body, her hair, the way she moved...

She let the water course over her, then beckoned to Glenn.

She's been with a lot of guys!

Yeah, so what?

He watched her wet down her hair. The temporary madness of sexual arousal was upon him.

So, this is just another fling to her. It's casual. And you know it.

He stepped into the tub, into the warm shower stream, and their hands were on each other immediately. They wrapped their arms around each other and kissed as passionately as two devoted lovers who haven't seen each other in months. If their bodies had been any closer together, they would have been merged into one.

The kiss ended and Sasha looked into his eyes. She looked... hopeful.

You don't feel about her the way you felt about Ashley.

And it was true. He looked at Sasha and saw a

beautiful woman. An amazing body. An exciting presence. He wanted to share his body with her. But... he had wanted to share *everything* with Ashley. Every part of him, including the intangible parts. Especially the intangible parts.

It won't be special. You know it. Not this way.

The rational part of Glenn was arguing with the part of him that just wanted to get laid... and winning.

He wanted something special, not just a sensation. Sasha was just a fling. The winter had come and the snow was deep. But no matter how badly he wanted to hibernate in her cave... he would leave again when conditions improved.

"I was so wrong about you," she was saying, looking into his eyes much too earnestly.

He wanted this, still. That had not changed. But there was more to think about than just pleasing himself... and her. "And Eric was wrong about you."

She started to smile, but then—"What...? What... did he say?"

Glenn adopted a grim look and began to rub her back. "He said you were a... self-absorbed slut." A lie. He had just lied to the woman he was about to have sex with.

She continued to look into his eyes, her expression falling into darkness. He looked right back. Then she did the last thing he was expecting—pulled him in and kissed him again, passionately. He kissed her back and hugged her tightly; this was exactly what he had been wanting... but life would go on after the sex was over, something people in estrus often seemed to forget.

The kiss lasted at least thirty seconds—it seemed she was trying to devour him. When it ended, she laid her head on his shoulder and began to tremble. As he held her, an uncomfortable warmth began to swell in his chest... he had hurt her. "I'm... sorry," he said.

"I tried to do things for him," she said, her plaintive

tone sounding very much like Craig's a few minutes earlier.

"Like what?" With their arms around each other like this, they could have been slow-dancing.

"You know... stuff guys like?" She raised her head, looked into his eyes again, then slowly rubbed her cheek against his. "Stuff I'm going to do with you..."

Glenn gave her a supportive squeeze. He wasn't sure what to think of all this... he had never expected such tenderness from THE Sasha Goldsmith—who would practically look for guys to seduce. Perhaps it was just a part of her method, though.

"She dumped him," Sasha went on, resting her forehead against his. "She's a... bitch. They had a good connection! He didn't deserve it. And he's still hurting after a month... almost a month. That's not right!"

Glenn pondered. Eric had been dumped most recently by... Sam. He had heard, however, that Eric had indeed deserved to be dumped. He hadn't heard why, though. Curse the inconsistent, unreliable gossip network. "So you comforted him," he said gently.

Sasha gave him a pleasant smile. "I did more than that, hon." She leaned in and kissed him again, this time with copious but gentle doses of tongue. He gave as good as he got... and he enjoyed it.

As they parted, he sucked on her bottom lip, and she moaned. "Give it to me," she said softly. "Please."

Glenn put his hands on her backside and lined up the necessary parts. He almost put them together... but stopped just short. "Mmf," said Sasha. "You tease."

Glenn smiled. "What else did you do?"

Her expression darkened again. "Inside me, now."

Glenn made an effort not to sigh or roll his eyes. Instead, he pushed her back against the wall, thinking back to Craig's instructions. "You'll get it when I say so. And I haven't said so yet."

"Oh, baby," she said, flaring her eyes at him. "I'll do whatever you say."

"You'll tell me what else you did."

She hugged him close again and spoke breathily into his ear. "Justice had to be done. You know. To the bitch."

He kissed her neck—a bit of encouragement. She giggled. "I came up with a plan. Something to humiliate her. And if it had... worse effects... that was just a bonus."

"Sounds terribly naughty. What was it?"

"I'll tell you after."

"After?"

"After you do what you know you want to do."

Again they rested their foreheads together. He did want it... at least, his body did. But he knew he shouldn't.

"You do know where to put it, right?" she asked softly. Her hand moved south to guide him.

He shouldn't... but he did. And just like that, with a flick of the hips, it was done and it couldn't be undone.

Craig sauntered out of the west end of the suite, the side that belonged to Cheryl, on paper at least. Now mostly empty aside from the furniture, a few cardboard boxes and a couple of shapeless pillows. No Ashley.

He could hear the shower running on Sasha's side. Then, suddenly, a powerful moan from Sasha. Craig smiled and nodded. Glenn seemed to be holding up his end of the plan... perhaps literally, even. Ashley had to be here; if Glenn was telling the truth, she had to be here. And if Glenn was lying... well, that meant a whole bunch of things that he didn't want to think about right now.

He looked around; the common area didn't offer many hiding places. There was the closet near the front door, which he had searched. And there was... the kitchen. A few of the cabinets in there were large enough, in theory, to fit a person inside. Hell, maybe even the oven...

Craig knew something was up as soon as he saw the kitchen floor. Bottles, jars and containers of leftover food were laid out on the linoleum, with enough space cleared so that the refrigerator door could be opened. Propped up against the oven were two translucent plastic shelves, the kind normally found... inside a refrigerator.

Craig felt a chill ripple through his body.

Glenn didn't feel like Glenn anymore. He felt as though he had stepped outside of himself somehow. Perhaps the real Glenn was still standing out in the hall, trying to think like an alpha male. Glenn Wallace wouldn't knock on a girl's door just for sex. He wouldn't lie to said girl. And he certainly would not use sex to get information. Yet he had done all of those things, and he was currently fu—err, having sex with—a girl who he had no intention of dating. He had no real interest in her at all, in fact. He would often think back to these events and wish it had never come to this.

Suddenly, she pulled away and turned around, looking toward the door. "Did you hear that?"

He was trying to pull her back. "It's okay. Come on—"

She shoved him—hard, with both hands. His feet slipped out from under him far too easily. Gravity took hold, and the back of his head met the bath spigot with agonizing force.

She had heard a clank—the sound of a bottle being knocked over. *Someone* was trespassing in her suite. The thought made her angry enough to forget about the sex, which *had* been pretty awesome. But no one had any right to come into her suite—HER suite—without her permission. She would hurt the motherfucker.

She had the bathroom door half-open before

remembering that she was naked. She lunged for her robe, without a glance toward Glenn, and continued on.

She was tying the belt when she reached the kitchen. There she saw... no. Just no.

Craig. And Ashley.

Only Ashley was limp. And her skin looked almost... grayish. Craig was holding her in his arms. The refrigerator door was wide open. A couple of knocked-over bottles lay at Craig's feet, including... the almost empty Petite Arvine.

This was it. The moment when her biggest mistake outgrew the tarp she had hastily thrown over it. It was bigger than life now... bigger than her life... and it would take twice as much effort to contain.

Craig reached out with one foot and pushed the door closed.

Sasha opened her mouth. Only by completely tensing her muscles could she keep them from trembling. She started to speak, but at first, all that came out was "Eh—"

Craig just stared into her eyes.

After a few tries, she formed the words she wanted: "I... told... you never... to come... back—here."

Craig gave her one last look, then turned and stepped toward the front door.

"Don't you have anything to say?" she asked, feeling frantic.

Craig paused at the door. "Words are wasted on you." With that, he pulled open the door and carried Ashley's body into the hall.

For a few seconds, Sasha couldn't move; her head felt like it was on fire; the world seemed too bright. She felt more exposed than if the entire school had seen her naked. And somehow, Craig was the worst person who could have discovered this. He was... important to her. She couldn't say how or why. They had never expressed affection for each other... not in the conventional way, at least. Mostly they had just insulted, argued and threatened each other with violence. And she had kind of hoped that he would make good on some of those threats. She cared about their interactions; she enjoyed them, even. There had always been so much energy between them... she had hoped that energy would catch fire and explode someday. She had fantasized about it often. But then he had found the body in her refrigerator. The way he had stared at her... as if he had never wanted the displeasure of seeing her again... she couldn't handle it.

The wine bottle. She picked it up by the neck. The door, she opened and into the hall. Her bare feet on the firm carpet. There was Craig's back, moving away. Her legs were moving. Her arm swinging. The bottle and Craig's head met. One of them broke. Maybe both. Liquid flew through the air. Someone yelled. Two bodies flopped to the floor.

Sasha was dizzy. She dropped to her knees. Breathing was difficult. Craig was trying to get up. He mustn't. She crawled forward. The thing in her hand was sharp. She jammed it downward with all her strength. Someone yelled again.

Then it was all quiet. The world settled... died... around her. There was nothing... but her breathing. And then she realized, she didn't like the quiet. But... she had made it this way. She had... killed the sound. She had... silenced everything.

Sasha sobbed. Tears formed, then began to run down over her cheeks. She cried, for all the things that she had done and all that had been done to her. She bawled, unrestrained, gasping for breath, at the feet of the man she had just killed.

Terrible things had happened because of her. Because of her plan. Because of her ridiculous revenge...

White Friday

November 26th, Thanksgiving Day ...yesterday.

As Eric knocked, Sasha stood back and admired the scarecrow decoration on the door. It was so aggressively average... as if someone had shoddily thrown it together as a joke. A parody of those homely-type folks who didn't think they needed money to be happy. Or perhaps a child had made it. Regardless, it would never pass as art.

She felt comfortable and, well... right. Not nervous at all. Her clothes probably helped. The emerald cashmere sweater from Neiman Marcus was a little too comfy—it didn't hug her curves at all. A size too big; she'd remember that. But it *was* comfy, so that was something. Underneath was a miracle bra that would perform at least one extra miracle tonight. The black slim-cut slacks from Macy's were just, well, standard fare. Of course, she spent 98% of her dorm time in bare feet, and tonight was no exception. Eric was in that blue flannel shirt he wore twice a week and those jeans he'd worn every day for, what... two weeks now? Guys.

After two knocks, the door opened and there stood Ashley, in sweats, looking slightly rumpled.

"Happy Thanksgiving!" they exclaimed, almost in unison. Eric held up the roast chicken—the most robust-looking one he could find at the supermarket, which wasn't saying much. Sasha, smiling widely, held up her bottle of Petite Arvine a little higher. ("Does that go with chicken?" Eric had asked. "Who cares? It's Ashley!" she had replied.)

"What... is this for me?" said Ashley.

Eric nodded. "Ya-huh!" piped Sasha. All she had to do was let them in. *Please just let us in for five minutes...* Sasha pointed toward the scarecrows. "Love this!"

Ashley looked awestruck. "This is amazing. Come in, come in..."

Sasha gazed around at the inside of the suite, half-shocked. It was so... clean and composed. It hardly looked lived in... but the added pillows and blankets in the living room sure looked comfy. And the decorative leaves gave the place a nice autumn look in shades of gold, orange, red, and brown. Not bad. Their TV, though... it was so tiny! And she thought The Bitch was supposed to have a wealthy family; perhaps not so much after all.

Ashley let the door close behind them. "Why, uh... what prompted this?"

Sasha set down the wine and pointed toward Ashley. "Because you should not be alone." She looked at Eric, setting the chicken on the table. "He has me, and you should have someone too."

Ashley raised her eyebrows and smiled. "What can I say, I'm content with the way things are right now... but thank you!"

"You don't have any family within... driving distance?" Eric asked.

"My aunt and uncle, but they're out of town right now." Ashley stuck out her arm toward the table. "Sit, please..."

Eric pulled out a chair and slowly sat. "Where's your family, your... the ones you're closest to?"

"Down in Florence and Sparta..." She clenched her hands together and gave them a wide-eyed grin. "Christmas break!"

Eric smiled warmly. Sasha let out a chuckle. "Where's your roomie?"

Ashley gestured vaguely eastward. "Over there. With her folks."

Eric nodded knowingly. "At the *estate*."

Sasha tried to keep the derision out of her face and voice. "Lah-dee-dah..." She sauntered toward the bedroom on the right and picked up the baseball bat that had been standing in the corner. "Is this the bat she threatened you with?"

Eric looked over. His eyes had the quality of a puppy being disciplined. "I never said 'threatened.'"

She ran a hand over it; solid, slightly worn... and very phallic. "No, but I understood your implications."

Ashley leaned against the chair facing Eric. "How are you doing? We haven't really talked since... that stuff."

Sasha concentrated on Ashley; maybe if she tried really hard, she could disintegrate the southern belle with beams from her eyes. She strained, but... it didn't happen.

Eric just shrugged. "I bounced back."

"Sure did," said someone. Eric and Ashley both looked toward Sasha, and she realized it had been her. "I can't partake of the wine," she said, setting down the bat, "but you guys totally should."

"Why can't you?" asked Eric, staring at her.

"Medication." Technically it was true; she *did* have meds that didn't interact well with alcohol, and sometimes she took them. She didn't usually follow that guideline, though.

"I don't drink a whole lot," Ashley said, smiling graciously. "Matter of fact, I ate a couple hours ago, otherwise I'd tear into this bird. You can get a drink from the fridge, though, if you want."

Sasha gave her best gracious smile and strode over to the refrigerator.

"We didn't interrupt anything, did we?" asked Eric. Sasha almost laughed. This was Ashley they were talking about... not to mention that she looked like a homeless person at the moment. Oh yeah, she was *totally* busy.

"Oh... just my annual Thanksgiving nap," said their host. Yeah, that sounded about right.

Sasha stepped right in front of the refrigerator so that her back would obscure anything she did. The first thing she saw inside was the clear pitcher with the blue top—a water filter. That might do. "I see I'm not the only one here who filters the water."

"Oh, yeah," said Ashley. "I haven't even tasted the unfiltered water here, I've used that since I moved in."

"It's yucky, trust me." Among the drinks, there were also some juice boxes... and a tall blue sport bottle, filled with what looked like water. Hmm. She grabbed it and held it up. "Is this taken?"

"That's Sam's," said Eric quickly.

"Oh." *Jackpot.*

"Mm-hmm," said Ashley. "She's got these little sports drink additives she's been mixing in with it."

Sasha turned, still holding the blue bottle. "Are those any good?"

Ashley looked at Eric, then shrugged. "Couldn't tell ya. Never tried one. Sam likes 'em, though."

"They come in different flavors?"

Ashley nodded. "Yep. Orange flavored, red flavored, blue flavored, purple flavored..."

Sasha grinned and turned back toward the fridge. *Quick and smooth. Quick and smooth. Quick and smooth.* She set the bottle on the shelf. Unscrewed the cap. Pulled an upright contact lens case from her bra. Opened it and dumped its contents, about a tablespoon of multicolored powder, into the water. Shoved the case back in her bra. Screwed the cap onto the bottle. Shook it gently and placed it back where it had been. Grabbed two juice boxes and whirled around with a jubilant look on her face. "I haven't had these since sixth grade!"

Ashley, now settled into a chair, smiled at her. She turned to Eric. "Any more, uh... brushes with campus security?"

"They seem so small now," Sasha said, approaching the table.

"Nope," said Eric, ignoring her. She'd remember that. "And you won't hear a peep out of my room. Not with these sensitive neighbors..."

White Friday

Sasha sat down, unwrapped the plastic-covered straw from one of the juice boxes and shoved it into the tiny hole. She felt like she was sitting in the cafeteria between Sarah Bailey and Liz Freemont. Any moment now, Fat Face Conklin would come waddling by with her pathetic old Garfield lunch box and pretend not to hear the insults hurled from the cool kids' table.

"They've been pretty lax about enforcing the so-called 'quiet hours,'" said Ashley. "I'm surprised."

"If they cared about enforcing rules, they wouldn't have made Craig an RA," said Eric.

Sasha giggled at the thought of Craig. He thought he was a cool kid, but was he really? Hmm...

Ashley: "You don't think Craig should be an RA?"

Eric: "He doesn't do anything but goof off with Glenn."

Glenn. Pfft. "Glenn is sooo gay, you guys..."

They both looked at her. She gave them each a surly glance. "What?"

There was silence at the table. Hmm. Apparently the conversation depended on her. "Well, look, Craig..." She felt her cheeks getting warm and she didn't care. She smiled involuntarily. "Craig is a handful... maybe more... but Glennnnn... he's got nothin'. Nothin' going on. He'll be a lot happier when he finally comes out, that's all I can say."

"Glenn is not..." started Ashley. "What, what makes you think he's... gay?"

Sasha stuck a thumb in her sweater and pulled down the already low-cut neckline. "He turned down this, twice. That's gay in my book. And most peoples' books..." She punctuated that statement with a long, hard suck, draining half of her juice box. Mmm, cherry.

"Jesus Christ, Sasha..." moaned Eric.

She looked at Ashley and gestured toward her man. "Eric here is a normal heterosexual. In fact, he made love to me three times the other night."

193

Eric gazed uneasily into the distance. "Two and a half."

Sasha reached out, gently, and took his hand. "Don't worry, dear. I always round up."

After a few seconds, his eyes met hers and he smiled reluctantly.

Ashley was leaning forward, staring at the tabletop. "You know, I'm not feeling well."

Finally. Sasha stood and grabbed her juice box. She'd been waiting for an out. "Maybe we should let you finish your nap."

"I'd appreciate that," said Ashley, looking up at her.

Sasha grabbed the chicken, in its plastic shell, and took it to the refrigerator. "I'll just put this in here for when you're hungry."

"Thank you guys," Ashley said.

"No problem," came Eric's voice. Sasha closed the fridge door and looked up to see him staring at her quizzically. "Let's hang out when you're feeling better."

"Yeah, yeah," Ashley was saying, sounding sincere.

Eric went straight for the door, opened it, and held it for Sasha. His eyes beckoned to her.

Sasha snatched her wine as she passed the table. "Maybe next time," she said, giving Ashley the sweetest smile she could muster.

"Mm-hmm," came the reply.

"Have a good night!" Eric called as the door swung shut behind them.

Click.

It was done. Sasha turned to him and smiled triumphantly. "Mission accomplished." Now they could relax... drink, play video games, make luxuriant love...

"Mission? What mission?"

He didn't understand. He might, after a while. Right now, her job was to get him smiling. He was much cuter that way.

12

Glenn was wet. He could have been lying at the base of a small waterfall... but the water flowing over him was warm. That seemed odd. He was just barely conscious enough to feel it.

Then the water turned cold, and Glenn became a lot more conscious. He emitted a high-pitched groan and scrambled into a sitting position. His hand found the smooth, solid edge of the tub and he opened his eyes.

At first the light seemed too bright. But after a few moments, he could see a human form crouched over him... and a face. It was Eric. He had an impressive purple bruise on his right temple.

Wait. There was something important he needed to address, and he thought he knew what it was. "What time is it? I need to know if my laundry is done."

Eric's expression was grim. "You've got bigger problems."

"No, really. If you leave wet clothes sitting in the washer for very long, they end up smelling musty. I don't want that."

Eric turned off the water; he seemed determined to look Glenn squarely in the eyes. "Put your clothes on," he growled, then stood and moved toward the door.

Glenn got to his knees, then started climbing toward a standing position. A sharp, fiery pain was drilling into the back of his head. He finally stood, fully—and braced himself against the two nearest walls as the world spun off its axis.

After a few nauseating seconds, the world managed to right itself. That was good. Glenn looked down for a moment and realized that he was pointing... but not with a finger.

Eric *had* looked uneasy...

People were talking outside, at least two, in hushed voices. One seemed to be Eric. The other was... female.

Glenn looked warily toward the door as he picked up his underwear. Had he done something he shouldn't have? Something with Sasha, perhaps? Although his bathroom had the same layout as this one, the pink towels and feminine hygiene products were quite obviously not his. And something told him that he was in Sasha's place... but he had no idea where that knowledge came from.

He put on everything but his shirt, which he grabbed before heading out to the common area. If he was in trouble, he might as well face it head-on, like the human battering ram he had played in high school.

Glenn sauntered into the common area. Eric was standing near the front door, leaning on one of the dining chairs. But right in front of him, sitting in one of the slightly-more-comfortable living room chairs was... Sam. She looked well-bundled in her thick winter coat, scarf and wool cap. He would have commented on how cute she looked... but her olive cheeks were wet with tear tracks that shone in the lamp light. As he approached, she looked up at him with big, frightened eyes.

White Friday

"Hey," he said, trying to sound gentle. Was she crying because of something he had done? He hadn't even known she was around.

"Hey," she said, with the same deflating tone Craig had used earlier.

"How are the roads?" He needed to know. Everything would be better once the police—and whoever else—had arrived.

"Not good," she said quietly.

Glenn realized that he wanted to hug her... but Eric was watching him intently... and Glenn remembered that he, himself, was shirtless. "How did you... get here?" He tried to sound genuinely curious as he pulled on his shirt.

"Snowmobile," said Eric, expressing no emotion whatsoever. Sam held up a silver key attached to a generic yellow keyring.

"Oh," said Glenn. He had not considered that, but yes, Sam's family could probably afford one... or several. "Cool." She looked up at him again, her eyes slightly less frightened but just as large and he thought, *I wonder if she's still single.*

They maintained eye contact until Eric said "Come on" a few seconds later. Glenn gave him an annoyed glance, then followed him into the hall.

Someone was lying face down in the hall. The top half of a wine bottle protruded from his lower back, left of center. A round pool of blood had soaked into the carpet beneath him, looking like the center of a bulls-eye. Bits of glass were strewn around him.

Glenn recognized the plain black t-shirt and the faded jeans with those frayed cuffs, just like his own. Because he and his roomie were the same height, and their 32-length jeans often dragged on the floor. And his roomie was on the floor. And he wasn't moving.

Glenn squeezed his eyes shut, tightly, hoping to somehow reset his vision so that he could see reality this time and not some frightening delusion. He opened them again and his roommate was still lying there. And his *head*... the *back of his head*, it was... *cracked open*... like a... like a... "What did you...?"

A voice beside him said, "Huh?"

Eric. Who had threatened Craig. Who Craig had thrown down the stairs. Who would have absolutely wanted revenge...

Glenn was launching himself at Eric, pushing him, smashing him against the wall with a reverberating THUD.

Eric was gasping, yelping in surprise and, hopefully, pain.

Glenn didn't bother drawing back; he drove his fist straight up against Eric's jaw. Eric's head bounced back against the wall and he yelped again.

He was emitting an "Ahhhh" of pain as Glenn drew back and hit him again, this time with a more traditional punch to the cheekbone. Eric stumbled and almost went down.

Glenn's knuckles were already beginning to ache, but he barely noticed it. He went after his quarry again. Eric was saying, "HOLD on! HOLD on!" but he didn't stop.

Glenn swung at him again. Eric flung out an arm and blocked it. "Stop!"

Glenn did not stop; he swung his other fist. Eric tried to dodge, but it still caught him on the temple. He let out a little "Augh!" sound, then charged, grabbing Glenn's upper arms and shoving him backward. "Stop!" he cried again.

Glenn pushed back, straining and groaning and baring his teeth. Their faces were less than a foot apart—Glenn had never been this close to Eric and had certainly never touched him. Fighting, he realized, could be a very intimate experience; sometimes you have to get close to someone if you want to destroy them. Suddenly, Eric stopped pushing. Glenn realized he was moving even closer—and then Eric swung his head down and—CLUNK.

Glenn saw a flash of light as their foreheads crashed together. He uttered an involuntary "Ah" and stumbled backward against the wall.

Eric was stumbling too, clutching his head. "God... DAMMIT! Why'd you make me do that?!"

Glenn did not answer. The pain in his forehead suggested to him, rather bluntly, that perhaps his skull had been cracked. He reached up, but felt nothing unusual. He realized, at that moment, that he had never been in a fight like this. Never had he simply attacked someone he knew just for the sake of hurting them. He didn't have much fighting experience in the first place. Before this month, the closest he had come had been helping to break up a tussle during a high school football game. But now, he was an instigator. Now he was really trying to hurt someone for selfish reasons. The disappointments and frustrations of the day had all come back to him at once—in fact, they had piled on like defenders making a goal line tackle. Ashley gone, their plans dashed, the ambulance taking forever, Craig lying motionless on the floor, Eric having invited himself into everything... and he could not quite remember what had happened with Sasha, but he somehow knew he had not gotten all he wanted. Not to mention the things he would not let himself remember.

This day, this Black Friday, was bursting with failure, more failure than he had ever encountered in a single month or even a year. So of course he was angry, and more... did he want to contribute to someone else's misery? Perhaps. But more likely, he was trying to say, *Okay, Black Friday. You want to trash my life, and the lives of people I care about? Fine. Let me help. I can do it just as well as you can! Let's fuck it up good!*

Eric was leaning against the opposite wall, staring at him. There was a sore-looking red mark on his forehead.

"Hit me," said Glenn. He had no intention of letting Eric hit him.

"N-no."

"Okay." Glenn stepped toward Eric, preparing to feint toward his head, then hit him in the stomach. That was when Black Friday decided to prove it had the upper hand.

WHAM. A giant, invisible hand shoved them to the floor, accompanied by the auditory equivalent of a frying pan to the ear. Chunks of drywall, ranging from pea-sized to fist-sized, rained down upon them. After that, the only sound was that of a blowtorch. A humungous blowtorch.

"Sam?" Eric's voice.

Glenn opened his eyes. The floor was littered with pieces of wall and other debris. A few of them looked like the white metal that made up the standard dorm ovens. Then he saw that much of the wall was gone, to the left of Sasha's door, right where her kitchen would be. All of it, illuminated with a dancing orange glow, from the fire spewing out of the gas line like water from a faucet. It was shooting directly into the apartment, where he and Eric had been just a minute ago. And Sam... where had she been?

"Sam!" Eric cried again.

Glenn climbed slowly to his feet. Something hit the floor and rattled; he and Eric both looked down. It was Sasha's prescription bottle, with the half-dozen tablets inside.

Eric stepped toward him; his expression and the firelight made him look like he was finally ready to fight. But he simply bent over and picked up the bottle. "You stole this," he said quietly.

Glenn just looked at him and shrugged. He couldn't think of a single word that would have made any difference. Instead, he took out his phone and dialed 9-1; the phone filled in the other 1 for him.

Things could have spiraled out of control from there. Glenn knew no way to stop the gas pouring out of the pipe, but he did know water would do no good on the flame. Eric, however, knew that each apartment had its own gas shut-off valve. Glenn attempted to inquire how he had learned this. Eric's answer: "Don't ask." Eric was also the only one, of the two of them, who had used a fire extinguisher before. Fortunately, each apartment came equipped with one of those, too. Eric calmly sprayed the white powder-ish substance at the base of all the flames and soon the apartment was filled with a pale fog. Glenn did not bother to ask in what situation he had gained that experience.

They had already dragged Sam a safe distance from the fire, frantically patting out the flames on her legs, but the severity of her injuries and her lack of breathing told them she was gone. She had apparently taken off her coat before the explosion, so Glenn had laid it over her as Eric prepared the extinguisher.

"Thank God the flames didn't reach the ceiling," Eric was saying, watching the white-ish powder settle.

"You seem to know a lot about fire," said Glenn.

Eric looked at him. Every muscle in his face seemed relaxed, and yet he looked angry. "I do."

Glenn had been wondering one thing since he came to in the tub, so finally he asked: "Have you seen Sasha?"

Eric reached into his pocket and pulled out the prescription bottle. "You mean the owner of this?"

"Well, she's the only Sasha in the building." He had felt quite dazed upon waking up. That, along with the soreness from fighting, had begun to fade into the background. His focus was on the three dead people, and the live ones unwilling to give answers.

"And what would you want with her?"

"Well, Fire Marshal Eric... I suppose that oven just exploded on its own." Glenn had a general idea of what had happened. He had seen the burst-open remains of at least two hair spray canisters among the debris, and he knew Eric had seen them too. "And I suppose Craig stabbed himself in the back."

Eric looked like he wanted to sneer. "So she's a murderer now?"

Glenn shrugged. "Someone here is. Three people don't die in one day without—"

"What do you mean, three?"

"I mean less than four, more than two."

"WHO?"

Glenn forcefully stuck out his right hand and raised his middle finger. "Craig." Raised a second finger. "Sam. And..."

And a locked chest in his mind sprang open.

"And?" said Eric.

"Sam..."

"That's two."

"No, but... Sam..." Memories of the shower were coming back to him like images from a half-forgotten dream. Sasha had wanted to hurt her... humiliate her... did Eric know? "Did you know she was coming back tonight?"

"No, she just... wanted to see how things were here, with the snow..."

"Oh. So... Sasha couldn't have expected her."

"No." Eric stared at him for a moment. "What are you suggesting now?"

"Just... I think Sasha may have had it in for her."

"You do, huh?" Audible venom in Eric's voice.

"Uh, yeah... has Sasha done anything odd lately?"

Eric looked around the ruined suite, then glared at Glenn.

"Before this."

Eric cocked his head. "Last night she wanted to visit Ashley and take her some food, for no apparent reason."

"And, did she?"

"We both did."

Glenn felt warm surprise spread across his face. "You two were there... last night?"

"Yeah. Problem?"

Glenn looked at the floor. "No... no."

"I didn't catch anything unusual. I think I would know if she did something shady."

"I think she's smarter than we give her credit for." Glenn was gazing at the hole in the kitchen wall, and the remaining foundation of the oven. "You didn't see her do anything strange... but that doesn't mean she didn't."

Eric reached for apartment 309's doorknob... then stopped to wipe the blood off his hand. He had insisted on looking over Sam's injuries one last time, to make sure she was beyond help. Then he had admitted, to Glenn's surprise, that he didn't know CPR. Eric had remained, kneeling over her body for a few more moments, then had silently replaced the coat over her and left Sasha's suite. Glenn had followed.

Now they stepped into the suite registered to two dead girls. Glenn felt more like a criminal this time, invading a personal space that had no one left to claim it. But he felt he should keep an eye on Ashley's belongings in Eric's presence... and he suspected that Eric felt the same way toward him and Sam's things. Chances were, neither of them had any desire to steal anything... but they couldn't help feeling a little overprotective today.

Eric's first move, after turning on the pervasive overhead lights, was to go for the refrigerator. Glenn watched from the dining area as he pulled out the roasted chicken, still intact in its plastic shell. He removed the lid and examined the bird closely for several seconds, then returned it to the fridge. He briefly looked over the other things in there—salad mix, yogurt, juice boxes and a few disposable bottles of water in the back. He closed the fridge door and gazed around the small kitchen, his face scrunched up in consternation. His gaze finally fell on... the two empty sport bottles, blue and purple, next to the empty water pitcher. He grabbed the blue one and held it up, an inch from his eyes, staring through the translucent plastic. Then he unscrewed the cap and overturned the bottle, shaking it over his outstretched palm. Glenn, about ten feet away, couldn't see anything falling out... but Eric sure seemed to see it.

The tip of Eric's tongue appeared between his lips and he pressed it, gently, against the middle of his palm. He retracted his tongue and gazed blankly into the living area; he seemed to have forgotten that Glenn was even there.

His mouth dropped open. "Oh wow," he said, barely loud enough for Glenn to hear.

"Yes?"

Eric finally seemed to remember that he was not alone. He glanced at Glenn, at the floor, then back to Glenn. He held up the blue bottle. "This is Sam's..."

"I know that." Glenn was getting impatient.

"It was full last night," said Eric with a grave look.

Okay, and...? Glenn waited for a few seconds, but Eric seemed to think no further explanation was necessary. "And what was that stuff you just... tongued?"

Eric held up the prescription bottle—Sasha's prescription bottle—and shook it.

Glenn thought for a moment. "Valium?"

Eric's eyes widened. "No. Not Valium. She stole these pills from me."

Glenn smirked. "Surprised?"

"Actually, yeah, because she tried them once and they made her nauseous." Eric's tone conveyed more than a little annoyance.

If the pills belonged to Eric, then they were probably some sort of illegal pharmaceutical. And Sasha couldn't handle them, but apparently she hadn't intended to use them herself... "She was apparently quite upset with Sam..."

"Apparently," Eric agreed.

They looked at each other for a moment, then Eric pursed his lips. "She, uh... said she didn't want to spoil the surprise."

"And you're still dating her."

Eric's response was a look that said *don't make me fight you again*. Considering that his own knuckles and forehead were still throbbing, Glenn had no intention to.

Eric stared silently at the counter top for at least ten seconds. Then: "She said 'mission accomplished.' I had no idea what she was talking about... I always thought, 'Sasha sees things differently from most people, but she's harmless'..." He moved toward the dining area, keeping one hand flat on the counter as though it were holding him up. Perhaps it was; he flopped into the first dining chair he reached. "I got dumped for... perfectly good reasons... Sam didn't do... anything wrong." His voice was slowly rising in pitch.

"Mmm," said Glenn, just for the sake of being supportive. The vague gossip he'd heard had just been confirmed—Eric did indeed deserve his dumping. No big surprise; Sam could do much better in the boyfriend department. Now he was just hoping that Eric could avoid what appeared to be an oncoming emotional breakdown. Maybe he could steer the conversation... "So those pills are... dangerous?"

Eric slumped back, looking almost relieved at the subject change. Still, one of his cheeks looked wet. "When

I first tried it... I was told different people get different side effects... dizziness... insomnia, paranoia... and some people end up feeling really dehydrated. So they drink a lot. I get that sometimes."

Glenn glanced around, uneasily, at all the empty water bottles; at least five of them in view. Within the past month, he had seen the local news report a fatal case of water poisoning—someone dead, just from drinking too much water in a short amount of time. It somehow disturbed the electrolyte balance in the brain. He had hardly believed such a thing possible.

Eric went on, looking at the tablets in the orange bottle: "I knew a guy... just some guy at a party... acquaintance, really... who took three or four of these within about an hour. He just kind of passed out... and never woke up. We all got the hell out of there when we realized he was... you know... gone..."

Glenn took a step toward him; he suddenly felt warm. "And yet you keep using them."

Eric's empty hand clenched tightly. "It's rare! I know a lot of people who have taken this stuff... and only one died!"

Glenn felt a surge of volcanic energy; he grabbed the edge of the table and shoved it toward Eric, pinning him against the back of the kitchen counter. "You may need to recalculate that number."

Eric stared up at him with wide eyes, his tightly shut mouth trembling. He looked frightened, vulnerable... hurt. Glenn didn't enjoy seeing Eric under normal circumstances, but he liked seeing him this way even less, because right now he looked... sympathetic. And the last thing Glenn wanted to do was sympathize with the irresponsible, substance-abusing, womanizing scumbag from down the hall.

Glenn gave the table a final shove and let go; Eric gasped in pain and surprise. At that, Glenn felt an instant pang of remorse, and the words "I'm sorry" almost escaped his lips... but he simply turned away instead. "Mission accomplished," he drawled. "And you were clueless..."

"Where *is* Ashley?" Eric asked in a tentative voice.

Glenn just stood there, staring in the direction of Ashley's room, wondering what to say. Finally he answered: "She's in my room, taking a nap."

Eric chuckled. He actually chuckled, and Glenn turned to look at him. "Seriously," said Eric. "Where is she?"

Glenn glared at him and thought of where he'd last seen her—the laundry room. And he had kicked an empty water bottle when he'd been down there last... "You had no inklings?"

"Well... I don't know! She's always... different! I can't keep track of her moods..." Eric trailed off and shook his head.

"Why are you two fighting, by the way?"

Eric just stared at him.

"Too much sex?"

Eric scoffed and smiled derisively. "You don't know Sasha that well."

Glenn shrugged. "Educate me." He sauntered back toward the table and sank into the chair opposite Eric. "You've been with her for almost a month, I'm sure you know everything." He would get the whole story out one way or another.

Eric gazed out toward the windows. Day was waning, but the snow seemed to generate its own eerie glow. "I don't think she'd ever let anyone know everything."

Glenn leaned forward and nodded. He had learned active listening skills from a certain Psychology student. "That's... sad, really."

"It is," said Eric. "Everyone needs someone who they can talk to about... anything. Sasha... doesn't have that."

"Not you?"

Eric crossed his arms and tilted his head down. "Hell no."

Glenn thought for a moment. "Bullshit. You two are close. You're, uh... sleeping together... she must confide in you."

Eric finally looked straight at him, incredulous. "You really don't know."

Glenn forced a chuckle. "No, I really don't. Come on, she walks around in a towel half the time, she's gotta be a fun girl to date..." Eric was shaking his head insistently... "I mean, the first time I saw her walking around in just a towel, I just about creamed myself!"

Eric stopped shaking his head and broke into a reluctant grin. "Yeah, yeah... you'd be forgiven. What about that bikini she wears outside, when it's warm?"

"Oh my God," said Glenn honestly. "I have to hold my books in front of my crotch when I see her in that. And, you know... *we're* the perverts, for looking at her, right?"

Eric rested his head in his hand. "Girls don't like being shown up like that. That's one of the reasons she has no one to talk to, I'm telling you!"

"So, what, am I not supposed to want her? Because I would totally switch places with you!"

"Oh, you're welcome to!" Eric spat. "Just watch out, that's all I'm saying."

"For what? STDs?"

Eric scoffed. "My idea of a nice gift? A new iPod. Her idea of a nice gift? Trying to harm someone who hurt you in the past. She thinks that's a *nice thing to do for her boyfriend*. She thinks that's a loving gift."

"So she did tell you..."

"She *bragged* about it. She was *excited*, and *proud*. Like... I dunno... like a little girl bringing home a good report card. And she thought I would be so happy about it..."

Glenn stared down at the table. He had nothing left to

say.

Eric pressed a fist against his forehead and choked out a brief sob. "I would've done something, I would've stopped it, but she wouldn't give me the details! She just said Sam would suffer... so I warned her... but... she still... and... *where's Ashley*?!"

Glenn looked at the purple sport bottle. He looked at the blue sport bottle. "Someone drank that. And had a bad reaction. Maybe felt dehydrated..." He looked around at the empty disposable bottles. "Someone who lived here."

Eric leaned forward and covered his face with both hands. He made no more sounds.

Then they heard it: banging. Someone was knocking on a door nearby. Knocking hard. *Must be an alpha male*, Glenn thought randomly. He froze in place, like an animal hoping to avoid detection.

"Glenn!" A strong male voice echoed in the hallway. "Glenn Wallace!"

He knew he should do something, respond somehow, but he remained still, waiting...

"Police!"

That was his cue.

13

One last time. Yes...

As Glenn stepped into the hall, Eric caught a glimpse of two men in dark blue uniforms. Eric had devoted a lot of time, thought, and effort to avoiding men in uniforms like that, so he remained still until the door swung shut again.

One last time. That phrase had popped into his head more and more during the past month. It implied that he was going to quit using Ex, even though he was pretty sure had made no such decision. Perhaps he was mistaken. Of course, he had become comfortable with the idea of "one last time" because it meant he *would* quit... but not yet.

Suddenly everything was blowing up. The fight with Sasha over her "revenge" plan. Glenn and Craig acting suspicious. The fight with Craig in the stairwell... although it was more like him getting his ass handed to him by gravity. Then he had awoken in some kind of action-suspense-disaster movie. Murders, fights, explosions... blood and pain... but not the kind of constant simmering pain that you could learn to minimize and live with. This pain was of the more immediate type. He was still trying to wrap his mind around the fight with Glenn, who had always seemed so docile. Glenn's calmness had always had a certain forced quality to it, though, as if he were constantly telling himself, *Choose your battles. Choose your battles. Choose. Your. Battles*. Well, Glenn had chosen that battle and he had won, as far as Eric was concerned. He had, after all, just seen the murdered body of his roommate and probably best friend. He had reason (not entirely bad reason) to assume that Eric had done it. So, his rage was probably justified. Eric tried to imagine how he would feel if one of his favorite people had just been murdered... then he realized he didn't have to imagine.

That was the real ice ball to the head. He had liked Craig well enough (before the stairwell incident), but didn't have any particular attachment to him. He didn't give a damn about damage to Sasha's suite, as long as she hadn't been in it at the time. But Samantha... he was going to do whatever it took to get her back into his life. He would have given up pills and weed and alcohol. He would have worked out. He would have become a legitimate straight-A student. He would have conformed himself to Samantha's image of a perfect man. And he had gotten so close to telling her that... and things had just blown up, literally and figuratively. He couldn't describe it further than that; the images were still raw in his head, like bloody slabs of meat lying on a butcher's counter. Suddenly all that time spent with Sasha became a waste; blank sheets of paper crumpled and thrown in the trash. And he recognized the time spent building a relationship with Sam for what it was: the best months of his life.

At least he had seen her... one last time.

Tears were welling up now, and overflowing from his eyes. He let it go, because it was fitting. It was right. And if he couldn't cry over the woman he had wanted to spend his life with, then he didn't want to be alive.

The prescription bottle still sat in front of him with some of those happy-looking pills still inside. He could take one... one last time. How many "last times" had he had recently? Well... about as many days had passed in the month. He remembered the note that had been slipped under his apartment door sometime around November 1st... he had spent the weekend at Sasha's, so he couldn't be sure of the exact day. But he had found it on Monday, the 2nd, a neatly folded sheet of journal-sized paper sealed in a security envelope. His first name written on the front. As one would expect, Ashley's handwriting was vigorously cute.

> Dear Eric,
>
> I've thought about our conversation. I've considered your reasons for taking that particular substance. I know you've had difficulties in your life; so have I. You're right about one thing: the effects of those pills are alluring. If I could make my life better with a pill, I would have taken them a long time ago.
>
> But here's the thing... they don't make your life better. They just make you feel better about your life as it is. So... what if your life is a dung heap? Why spend your time trying to feel good about something that stinks, when you can grab

a shovel and clean it up instead?

Just a thought.

~ Ashley

The idea had materialized that night: one last time. It meant he could love the pills and hate them at the same time. It meant days spent acting as if he was free of them... and nights, knowing he was not. It meant the party could continue, because it would end at some point. Just... not right away.

She was right; the pills made him feel good. That's why he took them, for God's sake! But his life wasn't anything resembling a dung heap. He got decent grades still, he got financial help from mom and dad, he usually had female companionship when he wanted it, which was most of the time. He didn't need the pills. He took them for fun. Just for fun.

But somehow, Ashley's note had awakened a voice within him; a voice he had not heard before. It calmly said things like "You'll be better off without Ex" and "Get that stuff out of your system before it hurts you." He usually just told it to shut up. Every time he swallowed a tablet, that authoritative voice simply said, "This is wrong." That was the most effective of anything it said. He never responded to it. All he could do was close his eyes and wait to feel good.

"One last time" was his response. It had become his mantra.

Now it seemed possible... no, likely... that his pills had hurt someone. Perhaps if he hadn't extended "one last time" into twenty-seven last times, things would be different. If he hadn't hooked up with Sasha, she wouldn't have stolen his pills. But then... he had only hooked up with her because Sam had dumped him... because of his pills. And Sasha had wanted revenge on Sam for dumping

White Friday

him... because of his pills. Ugh.

The pills had caused it all, really. If his life had come to resemble a dung heap in any way, it was because of them. In fact, he could probably remove all the dung from his life with a single swift stroke.

And suddenly he was in the bathroom; Sam's bathroom. The scent of her natural honey-based bath products caressed his nostrils... he had smelled those every day for much of the semester. His fingers were still wrapped around the orange plastic cylinder that rattled when he moved. He looked at the toilet. His lips were dry, so he opened the cabinet above the sink. The little yellow tube of lip balm stood on the second shelf in its usual place. He picked it up and pulled off the cap. The scent hit him before the balm touched his lips... so sweet... so smooth... succulent with flavors and feelings. They had shared it during their time together and now he felt everything he had ever felt with her. His eyes brimmed with stinging tears again, then overflowed.

He would never tell anyone that lip balm had made him cry... but he would have told *her*.

Now he was lifting the toilet lid, holding the prescription bottle over it. He could feel the wet tear tracks on his cheeks. He could do this. No problem at all. Push down on the white cap and turn. He did that. Turn the bottle sideways. He did that. Now tilt it just a little bit downward... and he did that. And pills began to plop into the water. One, two, three, four... and one left. One bright, happy orange tablet lingering. He turned the bottle upside down. *Plop*. He shook the bottle. He pounded on the bottom, just to make sure there were no more hiding inside. No more came.

They sat there at the bottom of the bowl, those happy, candy-looking pills. God, they still looked fun. Eric reached out, slowly and cautiously, as if unsure how his own muscles would perform. He touched the smooth white handle... and pushed it down. Forcefully. Held it down as the tablets swirled in their own little dance party. Then they were gone.

He could do this just fine. No problem at all... because he still had around a dozen of them. And he had a feeling that he'd need them before this business with Sasha was over.

The officer was tall, probably 6'5, and built like one of those offensive lineman Glenn had relied on back in high school. He looked Asian, but... no... Samoan. Yes. Glenn was fairly sure of that. He looked to be in his 50s and introduced himself as Officer Bailey. His partner, Officer Black, was a wiry white guy closer to Glenn's age.

Glenn led them silently to the third floor. He felt awkward and a bit ashamed, like a child leading his parent to some ridiculous mess he had made. Well, he had participated, hadn't he? And yes, there was a smear of blood on the wall that belonged to... him or Eric. He wasn't sure.

Officer Black immediately knelt over Craig's body and checked for a pulse. Bailey glanced at the hole in the wall and said something into his radio. Glenn didn't hear it; he was frozen, his arms crossed, watching Black examine his roommate. He felt like some judgment must be coming, like what he had gotten from his parents after putting the wrong kind of soap in the dishwasher at age 11.

Black looked at Bailey with wide, serious eyes and shook his head.

"Anyone else hurt?" Bailey asked in his husky tones.

"Yeah," Glenn said tentatively. His mouth was feeling a little dry.

Bailey stared, waiting for him to elaborate. "Where?"

"In the..." Glenn gestured toward Sasha's door. "Apartment." Black hurried into the suite. Glenn looked toward Bailey and made eye contact. "She's..." He shook his head.

Bailey nodded. He looked Glenn over, probably noticing the red, swollen knuckles and the spots of blood he had accumulated over the last half hour. Finally he pulled out a small, beat-up notepad and a pen. "Anyone else?" He sounded like he was trying to be patient.

Yes. Yes, there was someone else. Glenn closed his eyes. His mouth tightened into an anguished grimace. He nodded... then he heard the stairwell door opening. He opened his eyes and saw Eric stepping in to the hall, looking defeated.

Bailey raised a palm toward him. "Sir, please go back to your room."

"No, he—" Glenn felt strange, contradicting a policeman. It seemed necessary, though. "He was the one who found... Craig." He gestured toward his roomie.

"All right," said Bailey in an *I'm going to allow this* tone. He looked at Glenn. "Now, was someone else hurt?"

Glenn looked at Eric, then back at Bailey. His mouth opened and the word "Yes" spilled out. "Not here, though. All this happened... after... I called 911."

Bailey locked onto him with a *you're kidding me* stare for a few moments. Then, thankfully, Officer Black stepped out of Sasha's suite, his hands on his hips. "She's gone too," he said immediately.

Bailey nodded at him. "How do things look in there?"

"Looks okay. Fire's all out, gas turned off."

Glenn caught Eric's eye and gave him a grudging nod of respect. He didn't want to think about how bad things could have gotten without him there. Eric smiled a bit, not a private smile, either.

"Where's this other person?" Bailey jotted a few things in his notepad and looked back at Glenn.

Where was she? Um. Glenn felt a chill run through his body. "I don't know." And suddenly he was being squeezed between Bailey's incredulous stare and the wall. He felt the wall would be easier to break through. "I've been trying to find her."

"How badly is she hurt?" Black asked, his voice almost gentle compared to that of his partner.

"She's... she's gone."

"Gone where?" Bailey asked flatly.

Oh, holy shit. I can't even use the same expressions as you guys? You won't even give me that little bit of slack? "Come on! You know what I mean! She's dead!" Glenn turned away in disgust. He rarely showed his anger like that, but he couldn't hold it in any longer.

"Yeah, okay. Sorry." Bailey's voice had softened from a steel plate into steel wool. "Was that the person you initially found?"

Glenn's "Yes" was barely above a whisper.

"What's her name?"

He knew without looking that Eric was staring at him, waiting. He had probably figured it out already, but hearing the name, stated as a fact to an authority figure, well... it couldn't get much more real than that, could it?

"What's her name?" Bailey repeated, somehow maintaining the same tone.

"Ash-ley." And there she was, laying curled up on the elevator floor like she was asleep. He closed his eyes, but that only made the picture more clear. She was pale. She wasn't breathing. And there was just... less of her. In that worn Alabama sweatshirt, so old that the crimson fabric had begun to pill. And then he was curled up with her on one of the standard single beds, fully clothed of course, and it wasn't wishful thinking, not anymore, it was real... or, at least, it had been.

"Last name?"

Glenn sighed. "Freeman."

He had wrapped his arms around her not twenty-four hours ago... she had been breathing, her eyes had been focused on him... and it had been wonderful. How inhumanly cruel that the memory of that had now become more painful than anything else he could remember. The extraordinary warmth of their touch had been extinguished in such a short time.

"What do you think happened to her body?"

There was nothing he could say; he had no idea anymore. He opened his eyes and turned, tentatively, toward the others. Eric made eye contact with him, his expression subdued. After a few moments, Glenn dropped his gaze to the floor. "I don't know."

"It had to be Sasha," said Eric. Glenn looked up in surprise; Eric gave him a furtive glance. "She's been... unstable." He pointed toward the glass protruding from Craig's back. "That was her wine bottle." He pointed toward the hole in the wall. "That's her apartment. And her oven. Exploded with..." He glanced at Glenn once more. "...her hairspray cans. Besides, I don't think there's anyone else here."

Bailey was still jotting down notes. "That's a lot to digest."

"Does this Sasha have psychiatric troubles?" asked Officer Black.

Eric nodded.

Bailey and Black exchanged a sober look. "You could hide a body anywhere with this snow," said Black.

"Oh God." Another chest had sprung open in Glenn's mind. He quickly reached toward Craig's body. Black moved to stop him. "Keys," said Glenn, stopping. "He should have... a big-ass... ring of keys in his pocket. He was an RA."

"Building keys?" Bailey's eyes suddenly looked quite large.

Black knelt, patted Craig's pockets and raised him slightly to look underneath. "They're not here," he said, rising.

"Well there you go," said Bailey.

"What rooms can RA's access that other students can't?" asked Eric.

Glenn looked at him and smiled a little. They were both starting to act like amateur detectives. "Housing office... maintenance room..." And there was a flash of energy in his chest. *This is it*, it was saying, *get going!* Yeah, he knew where Sasha had gone with those keys, and probably with Ashley. "The roof."

They followed Officer Bailey up to the fourth floor of the stairwell, where a ladder attached to one wall led to a metal hatch in the ceiling. The hatch was visibly ajar, with snowflakes drifting in. "Okay guys," said Bailey. "Stay back and let me handle this. I assume this Sasha isn't very big?"

Glenn and Eric looked at each other. "Five-eleven," said Glenn. "Skinny..." He shrugged and looked at Eric, who nodded.

"She don't do PCP, right?"

Glenn and Eric exchanged another, more confused look, then slowly shook their heads.

Bailey smiled. "We're good, then." He grabbed the ladder and started climbing. His voice boomed: "Sasha! Police! I'm coming up, don't try anything!" They watched as he ascended, pushed the hatch open and just barely fit his broad shoulders through.

Then they heard the sound of a home run being hit, and 250 pounds of Samoan police officer dropped twelve feet and crumpled to the floor. The landing shuddered.

Glenn and Eric rushed to his side. Fortunately his head had not hit the floor or the nearby railing, but the right side of his forehead did bear a big red splotch from... something. He seemed to be unconscious, but he was still breathing.

White Friday

After a few moments, Eric rolled Bailey onto his side. Glenn gave him a quizzical glance. "He could have a concussion," said Eric. "Which means possible vomiting. Shouldn't be on his back." Glenn nodded; he had heard that before, he just hadn't thought of it.

Snowflakes drifted down toward them. Glenn turned his gaze up toward the hole in the roof. He thought he heard ragged breathing from above. He rose and climbed onto the ladder.

"Don't," came Eric's voice, quietly. Glenn looked down at his face—he meant it. He really did.

Glenn replied in a hushed tone. "She's up there... with Sasha." He climbed, squeezing rung after corrugated rung, rising into the frigid air. Not officially winter, no... but it was here in spirit. He stopped just before his head could breach the opening of the hatch. A large snowflake landed on his nose. He shivered... but he wasn't that cold, not yet. "Sasha? Is that you?"

"You can't stop me, Glenn!" Her voice was trembling.

He hung there for a moment, thinking. "I can't—I don't want to stop you."

A pause. "What?"

"I just... I want to see you." And he did, kind of. He had a sense of some... recent intimate contact with her. Part of him wanted to continue that.

Silence from above.

"May I see you, Sasha?"

No response. Glenn put his foot on the next rung, grabbed the edge of the hatch and climbed up.

The roof was covered in white. The cloud-covered sky was a dingy gray, except to the west, where a burst of pink had begun to bloom. Dark mountains to the east and west. The air was shockingly chilly, but at least it was still. And in the daylight that had just begun to wane, he saw Sasha. Against the setting sun, her sideways silhouette looked like a scrawny, limbless tree. But after a few moments, he could make out details: jeans, a sweater and a brown leather jacket. Her hair hung limply. Her face looked pale... except her cheeks and around her eyes—those were crimson. She held a baseball bat at her side.

"Why come up here?" he asked, stepping into the two feet of wet snow.

"I'm not sure..." Her voice, half-hearted, drifted off. "I'm not... entirely convinced that this isn't a dream..."

He stepped toward her; her only move was to turn her head toward him. "So... a lucid dream, perhaps?"

She was looking straight at him. "Maybe..."

He was slightly excited and he still wanted her... but he also had to get that bat out of her hands. Two birds with one stone, perhaps...

"Dream or not... are you okay?"

She looked at him for a moment, then ran a hand up over her face. "I'm, uh... I'm..."

He took another step toward her. There were only inches between them now.

"I'm not," she finally finished, her gaze drifting from his eyes, down over his shirt... "I'm not," she sobbed.

All at once, he extended his arms and she fell into them. Her face rested on his shoulder. Her hands wrapped around his waist.

Her hands... empty.

"I'm not," she was saying. "Oh, God, I'm not... I need help... I need someone... if this is a dream, it's been a horrible one..."

He squeezed her. "All of it?"

She was quiet for a moment. "Huh..." She raised her head and pressed her forehead against his. "You're right... some of it has been... wonderful..."

She kissed him, quickly, playfully. And an ambulance, lights flashing, pulled into the parking lot, heading toward their building.

White Friday

Sasha took his hand and pulled him toward the front edge of the roof. "Come on, let's watch!"

She half-dragged him to the edge, fifty feet away. He looked around as they went. There weren't any obviously suspicious piles of snow, but it was naturally deep enough in some places to easily hide a body. She stopped a foot from the edge and looked down. He pressed up against her rear.

The ambulance had pulled up at the main entrance behind a police car and a large snow plow. Sam's snowmobile was parked in the area of one of the parking spaces. None of the asphalt surface was visible, only white. Sasha turned toward him suddenly. "Isn't this exciting?"

"You're excited?"

"Mmm," she said, putting her hands on his shoulders. "In many ways..."

He smiled. She kissed him. He kissed back. This scenario did seem to be affecting him. On one level, he wanted to put it to her right here, in the snow, and frostbite be damned. On another level, though... that could never happen. Not now. The first level argued back: it was now or, perhaps, never. So, he kissed her deeper and hugged her tighter. Her tongue slipped into his mouth...

His eyes closed, an image came to him: Ashley, looking lovely and cute in her sweats... eating turkey pot pie... smiling at him...

He opened his eyes and gently pulled away.

Sasha smiled at him. She took his hands in her own. "You think we could do it up here?"

Glenn stared into her eyes... and he could not think. She was lovely, and fun, and affectionate... and so very good at sex. And part of him kept saying *that might be enough, that might be enough!* He knew very well what part it was coming from, though. Because he had had sex before, and he knew that feelings could change. She might look amazing as long as the blood was being diverted south, and every word she said might be the gospel truth... but after the orgasms, after their energy was sapped and their urges fulfilled... would she look the same to him? She would still be lovely, fun, good at sex... but that would not be enough.

"Listen... you are attractive, God knows... and difficult to resist. And... amazing, when it comes to sex. But that's just a piece of life... a fraction... and I think... I mean, I want to know all of you, not just your body and... the amazing things you can do in the shower..."

"What about in bed? Ashley's bed? You were pretty focused on my body then."

"That... wasn't me." Why? Why tell the truth now? Because the baseball bat was fifty feet away, for one. And because, dammit, the police were here and and the EMTs were here and there was no having sex on the roof. Not here, not now. It was over. Time for real life to resume.

"Not... you?"

He shook his head. "I'm sorry."

She let go of his hands and turned toward the edge for a moment. "It wasn't Eric, I know that," she said with derision. She looked back toward Glenn. "You're lying. Who else is here?"

Glenn just stared at her, trying not to wince.

Her expression changed as it came to her. "Oh, God... *Craig*?"

Glenn could only smile painfully. Why had he said it? WHY?

Sasha wrapped her arms around herself, slowly turning toward the edge again. "Oh, God... oh, Craig..." She stared out into the distance.

Craig? *Craig?* Craig...

Their energy... it *had* exploded. Only she hadn't *known*

it. And it *had* been amazing. It had been... *nuclear*. And then she had ended him. No more arguments. No more threats. No more heat.

She'd had no choice!

"Where'd you put her, Sasha?!" It was Eric's voice, wasn't it?

She whirled. Glenn did too. And there was Eric, near the hatch, holding the baseball bat.

It was too much. From Daddy saying "Relax, you'll enjoy this" when she was twelve, to mother, who seldom said more than "Those pills working for you?" to all the men (some technically boys) who had made love to her despite not really caring about her at all... and more... it all added up. And the bill had come. It was too much, more than she could ever pay for. Now, two amazing people were gone, wiped from the earth... one of whom she could have really loved... all her fault. Added to the bill. She couldn't afford it, but she would still have to pay.

If this was a dream, it had to end. If it was real... same solution.

She couldn't do it alone. She never wanted to be alone—never again. So she grabbed Glenn's hand.

The edge was right there. So open, so easy. She could feel gravity calling.

She jumped.

Since childhood, she had always been attracted to ledges and balconies and any high, open places. She liked to gaze down... lean over the edge... imagine what it would feel like to fall. The thought exhilarated her. Just a quick leap and the thrill—or so she assumed—of falling, being unattached and weightless...

It was everything she had thought it would be. She was in the air, free of the building, almost flying, it seemed. No ground except that four stories below. She kicked her legs wildly. It was pure life. She was feeling... everything. And Glenn was with her.

Flying together.

Except... no. He was resisting. He was pulling. She lost her grip on him.

Still flying.

But Glenn was not with her. She was alone.

Falling.

Alone.

14

There was a crunching sound below, like stepping on a cockroach only a thousand times worse. Glenn's eyes were fixed on the wall in front of him; he probably wouldn't have looked down if he could have. The ledge was cold. Snow was everywhere. Holding on was all he could do... forget about pulling himself up.

This was it. The pull of gravity versus his cold, weak fingers. Even though there were ten of them, and he had those highly-lauded opposable thumbs, he knew which force would win in a prolonged struggle. The space between him and the ground, the lack of anything to put his feet on, made things feel so... final.

Then Eric was there, grabbing his wrists, grunting, dragging him up over the edge.

Glenn let himself lay there for a minute at the edge. He could still feel the open air under his lower legs, but there was something solid under him now and things were no longer so... final. He had time again.

But... Sasha. She had no time left. Glenn pounded a fist against the roof. They hadn't pushed her off, no... but they had helped.

Eric had dropped into a sitting position nearby, panting. Glenn looked up at him. "Dude..." he said.

Glenn shook his head. There were no words.

He gazed around the roof slowly, just trying to take it in. It was so much larger than he had imagined... but then, he hadn't really considered the fact that the building had a flat roof. Such an expansive, mostly empty space. But there, in the distance—near the hallway branch on the west wing... there was something pink. Neon pink.

He climbed to his feet, realizing that he felt okay, if a little shaky. He began to trudge through the field of white toward the pink. He heard a "What..." from Eric, and a few moments later, there were footsteps crunching in the snow behind him. The snow was wet and heavy—very good for packing.

It took about two minutes to reach the western edge of the roof. The pink, red and orange flare behind the clouds indicated that the sun was nearing its rest. It was really quite beautiful, so much so that Glenn almost stopped to admire it. Almost.

The pink thing was a sleeping bag, bunched up and, perhaps, forgotten. Two kinked and slightly tangled extension cords lay curled up with it. Less than a foot away, the snow looked much more packed than it did anywhere else—snow that had been pushed down by hands... covering something. Protecting something.

Glenn drove his bare hands into the packed area and began shoveling away snow. Handful after handful, carving a crater in the bed of white... until something began to show through. Something crimson. He pushed away snow and touched it... a red sweatshirt.

After two more minutes, he had completely uncovered her. Wet from the snow. Her gold hair impossibly messy and plastered against her skin. Her limp flesh had a tinge of gray. Her lips, blue.

He had attempted to hide her just to avoid something like this. Hoping for some dignity. Even after death, she had been treated worse than she could have ever deserved. He picked her up in his arms, just as he had in the elevator so long ago... only this time with a practiced ease.

Eric, his face ashen, stepped forward, reaching toward her gently. "Oh no..."

"Don't touch her," said Glenn.

Eric looked at Glenn's face and backed off immediately.

Was it okay to remember now? Perhaps not. Did he have a choice? Definitely not.

"I AIN'T GONNA STOP! WHERE IS HE?! WHERE IS HE?!"

He climbed the stairs as quickly as his legs would allow. He reached the fourth floor landing. He hooked his hands into Scruffy Man's wool-lined shirt-thing. He pulled with all his upper body weight. Scruff stumbled backward. Glenn swerved him toward the stairs, hoping and fearing for the fall that might come.

He had caught Scruff by surprise, and maneuvering him, at this moment, proved rather easy. With one final shove, Glenn released his grip. He instinctively turned back to see just who the man had been terrorizing.

Ashley, seated in the corner, looked up at him. There was blood on her face. There was fear in her eyes... enough for both of them.

"Hey!"

Glenn turned. Scruff was ascending, advancing on him.

Ashley. It's Ashley. Glenn launched himself. A rush of cold air shot up through his torso as he realized what was coming. Something hard struck his chin, perhaps it was a fist, but his momentum did not flag. He crashed into

Scruff. They locked onto each other, tumbling, each sharp step digging into one or the other as they rolled.

They hit the landing between floors. Glenn landed on top, his opponent's fingernails biting into the back of his neck. He found his knees, rose onto them, pulling his enemy a foot off the floor, then slammed him down again.

Scruff's arms slackened for a moment and Glenn pulled himself away, throwing a quick kick to cover his escape.

Scruff, growling, rolled onto his side and slowly climbed to his feet. Glenn watched, unable to think and unwilling to move. *He'll go back after her, just wait, he'll go back up—*

Glenn stepped toward Scruff, hands held out to push him back. Then something big and hard came out of nowhere and smashed into the left side of his jaw. Glenn staggered sideways, straight into the wall, feeling like his face was about to fall off.

Holy Hell, that was a fist!

Suddenly he felt like he was stuck in a vat of glue. He slowly raised a hand and used it to push himself away from the wall. Scruff was moving slightly faster, moving toward him.

Glenn lowered his head and bull-rushed his opponent, feeling like a running back once more. The fist-shaped thing crashed against his temple this time, then two hands grabbed Glenn's shoulders and shoved him aside, toward the big window.

Glenn's feet lost contact with the floor; he went down on his butt. Shoes were squeaking on the floor; Scruff was heading back toward the fourth floor landing. Back toward Ashley.

Glenn clenched every muscle in his body. Some of them cried out in pain, but they all responded. He got up. He reached his quarry mounting the first step. He grabbed the back of Scruff's shirt and tugged.

Scruff whirled, swinging his fist. Glenn spun away. The big fist-thing sailed past him for once. Scruff's momentum had turned him back toward the big, sectioned window.

Glenn jumped up and wrapped his arm around Scruff's neck from behind. Scruff grabbed at him, trying to pull away. Glenn surged forward like a running back pushing his blocker toward the goal line...

CRASH. Scruff's face broke the plane, shattering one of the window sections. He screamed. Frosty air enveloped them and Glenn felt something warm and wet on his arm. He pulled them back and let go, instantly wondering if he was still being too merciful.

But Scruff fell to his knees and scrambled toward the down flight.

Well, as long as he's going... Glenn rushed forward and kicked Scruff in the gut, sending him rolling down toward the third floor. Moments later there were receding footsteps, and his groans slowly died away.

Glenn gave one final look toward the stairway below, then dashed back up to the fourth floor landing. Equal measures of surprise and relief greeted him—Ashley still sat there in the corner, looking straight up at him. She hadn't fled, as he'd thought she might. He tried to give her a smile, but it didn't feel right, so he simply said "Wow."

Ashley reached over and patted the floor next to her.

Glenn looked into those big eyes and couldn't resist; he dropped to the floor beside her.

"That was pretty impressive," she said.

He turned his head to look at her—it hurt. She had wiped most of the blood off her face. "Which part?"

She smiled. "Oh, it was all pretty good, but the finale was the best."

"Oh," said Glenn. "Yeah. I, uh, was pretty sure he'd try to hit me again, so I... used it against him. I *can* learn when I need to." A soft chuckle issued from Ashley's lips. "In high school, Coach Ware made us read The Art of War. We thought it was so cool to carry around a book of war tactics, even though we didn't need them for class. Reading it, though, was something else. Anyway, there was something about energy and momentum... I used it occasionally when running the ball... if I stuttered or twisted at just the right moment in just the right way, I could make a guy miss me entirely. Using his own momentum to take him out of the play." He jerked away as something touched the side of his face, then he saw it was Ashley's fingers. He relaxed; she ran her fingers, with their unpainted nails, down his temple and along his cheek.

"Good to know your memory is intact," she said with a hint of charm.

"Ha ha," he replied. *Keep it up, keep it up, please keep it up...*

She dropped her hand back to the floor and sighed.

"Are you okay?" he asked.

She nodded.

He tilted his head toward her. "You remember who I am?"

She reached over and smacked him on the shoulder. "Come on, now. You're the guy who has that crush on me."

Glenn looked over and made eye contact. It was the hardest thing he had done today. "You know your stuff."

She gave him a sweet smile. And didn't look away.

Now to do something even harder. He began to raise his arm, hesitated for a split second, then went for it, wrapping his arm around her shoulders. She inched closer and rested her head against him. He had seen her many times but had never touched her until now. Eyes can play tricks, but hands never do. If seeing is believing, then touching is experiencing. Wrap your arm around someone and they become a part of your world in the most concrete way possible.

They sat there like that, expanding each other's worlds, for a few minutes. Then Glenn spoke: "You know him?"

"I thought I did," she said.

Glenn considered the possibilities suggested by that answer and instinctively squeezed her a little. "Maybe we should get you back to your place."

After a moment, she answered. "Can we go to your place instead?"

Now different possibilities were running through his head, but he paid no attention to them. "Sure."

Three hours later, Glenn stepped into the doorway of his bedroom. It was dark, but a bit of light from the common area filtered in. Ashley lay curled up on his bed, in her jeans and hooded sweatshirt. She had cleaned up her wounds in his bathroom, though a black eye was slowly developing. He had gone to the dining hall and brought back dinner for both of them. Then she had asked if she could take a nap on the couch. He had suggested the bed because, honestly, the standard dorm couches and chairs weren't exactly designed for human comfort.

Glenn ran the heel of his thumb along the left side of his jaw. It had become very sore, understandably, and he thought he had seen a bruise starting to emerge. He still wasn't quite sure what had happened that afternoon. He had come back from class... there had been an altercation... and he and Ashley had somehow broken through the barrier that had previously separated them. Over the entire semester, she had touched his arm two or three times, casually... but she had hugged him three times in the past three hours. Hourly hugs... that was a rate he could get used to. He wondered how long she had known about his feelings... well, it didn't really matter. She seemed okay with them; in fact, it seemed as if she might even feel the same way.

And all he had done was to rescue her from a crazed attacker.

Yes. A crazed attacker. An assault. A sudden rescue. They had experienced danger and adrenaline together. He was no Psychology major, but he knew experiences like that could play with one's emotions. Maybe she had liked him for a while... and maybe she just felt warm and fuzzy toward him now because he had saved her from her vicious... ex?

Or maybe she actually liked him and the tension had finally been broken. Time had a way of sorting out these things. Probably the most reliable way.

He thought he saw her stir in the low light. Dammit. He had been trying to avoid waking her. Ashley rolled over and looked at him. She may have smiled.

"Feeling okay?" he asked.

"Yes. Just a little sore."

"Do you need anything from your place?"

She thought for a moment. "Nah."

He leaned against the door frame. She laid her head back on the pillow.

"Sam might wonder where you are."

"She went home for the weekend."

"Huh."

Ashley shuffled to the side and patted the empty space on the bed next to her. Glenn wanted this... but how much of it was genuine and how much inspired by the emotions of the day?

"It's okay," she said as he hesitated.

Okay. Perhaps he was thinking too much. He approached the bed and sat on the edge.

"I'm not talkin' to your back."

Well, he did want to lay down next to her. So he did. Carefully. They couldn't both fit on the single bed without touching. First their shoulders and arms met. Then their hands brushed against each other. Then their fingers were entwined.

"Don't worry," she said. "It's way too early for me to be taking advantage of you."

He smiled in the darkness. "Early tonight, or early... in our relationship?"

She laughed softly. "Take your pick."

He laid there for a few moments, enjoying the sensations, then he had to ask. "Was he your husband?"

With very little hesitation: "He was."

"He, uh... hurt you before?"

"Mmm-hmm."

"Well that's not right."

She was silent for a while. "I don't want to be alone tonight."

"Hey, this is my place. I'm not going anywhere. Except the floor."

She rolled onto her side and looked at him. "You don't have to."

He looked into her face, though he couldn't make out her exact expression. "Why don't I?"

She took his hand again. "This is why."

He smiled and squeezed her hand. "This makes me happy. But I'm going to sleep on the floor. If you still feel this way tomorrow, then we should talk."

"Okay."

"If you don't, then... you don't have to say anything. It's cool."

"Wouldn't the couch be more comfy, though?"

"You'd think so, but no."

So he slept on the floor near the bed. And the next day, they did talk. That made him forget all about the stiff back the floor had given him.

Ray Jordan

There it was, one of the memories he'd been holding back since seeing Ashley lying in that elevator, lifeless. Letting it play back through his mind caused him pain, of course, but afterward there was also a kind of relief. A feeling of... getting it over with. Perhaps the knowledge in his mind that he was holding it back had caused more tension than the memory itself. Perhaps in the future, whenever something wanted to come forth, be it thought, feeling or memory, he should just let it come.

And so the thought came to him as he was sitting on his couch in his living room, trying to relax: just how much had changed today? Well... a lot. That was the closest he could come to quantifying it. The extent of what had happened probably wouldn't hit him until tomorrow, or maybe even Monday, when classes resumed. He wondered if Scruff... *Kyle*... would venture back, or if someone would tell him that both his ex-wife and his child had passed on. He would have to find some new people to harass—and he probably would, that was the really sad part.

And who would tell Glenn that two of his favorite people were gone? Fortunately, no one would have to bear the burden of breaking that bad news to him. What would Monday nights be like without Craig? No more getting Chinese food and watching the game. No more Nerf gun fights. Never again would he hear Craig pacing through the suite, trying to help some confused resident with their problems. He would never again encounter Ashley's adorable face in the hallway. No more lazy Sunday afternoons in each other's company. Never again would he wrap his arms around her... something he had just begun to get used to. Craig and Ashley... pillars of Glenn's life. Load-bearing pillars? Would life collapse without them? Maybe. He could only wait and see. It was very possible that those two were the only reasons he found life at this school bearable. In fact, with those two around, it had been pretty damn wonderful. Take away two people, and wonderful could so easily become miserable. Would it, though? He could only wait and see.

Then the door opened, thankfully, to save him from his excess thinking. In came Eric, carrying two bottles of beer, acting casual as if there were no police officers in the hall. He flopped into the adjacent chair and handed a bottle to Glenn. "*Hondo?*"

Glenn glanced at the TV. He had honestly forgotten it was on; his thoughts had drowned it out. The John Wayne marathon had gone on without interruption, and now the movie appeared to be *Hondo* indeed. "Yup." The beer was so cold. Like the snow he had dug. He twisted off the cap and swallowed a mouthful. Today was one of those days when the taste of beer was welcome. "You've had tough times..." Glenn began.

Eric grunted.

"Times like that... have you ever felt like you needed some... physical comfort?"

Eric swallowed his beer thoughtfully. He looked at Glenn, then at his own bottle... then back to Glenn. "You mean sex."

Glenn grunted.

"Totally."

Glenn nodded, looked away. "I can't believe I did that... with her. I mean... any other time, no."

Eric swallowed several mouthfuls of beer, staring at the TV, before responding. "Hey, I'm in the same boat... only I'm the captain. It was Sasha, man. I mean, that's what she *did*... she seduced people. She got to me when I was vulnerable... and the same with you."

"I went along with it, though." It disturbed him, how easily he had succumbed, despite his ability to resist her in the past. Today, it had been almost as easy as falling off a log.

"Comfort. People who have just lost something wonderful... they want comfort. They *need* comfort. It's normal, I think... I mean, from what you told me, it sounds like you almost had... *it*."

Glenn furrowed his brow. "It?"

Eric nodded and let his gaze sink to the floor. "Look, I admit, most of the girls I date..." He held up his beer. "They're like this stuff. Fun, appealing, intoxicating... but essentially, a mild form of poison."

"Mild?"

Eric hesitated. "All right. Sasha was Everclear."

"Taken intravenously."

Eric stared at him. "You done?"

"Yup."

"Good. Anyway... you can't live on that. I certainly couldn't... not for lack of trying. But Ashley was like... the antidote, for you."

Glenn nodded. Unexpected depths from Eric were becoming somewhat... expected. He *had* experienced "it"... that thing everyone chases, that satiated feeling, that happy contentment. Should he not feel grateful because he'd had it for "only" a couple weeks?

"Some guys never find a girl like that," Eric was saying. "Some guys find one and... fumble her away. And maybe you were her antidote, too."

Glenn stared... not at the TV, but at the wall. Something else wanted to come forth. "For Thanksgiving, she made this big pot pie with turkey... lots of turkey... we couldn't help but eat the whole thing. And while it was cooking, she asked me to go look in her sock drawer. She said something in there might interest me. Something that she... couldn't do without... something her roommate would never approve of. So I'm thinking 'jeez, what now? What's the next Ashley secret?' It was a can of cranberry sauce... the cheap jellied kind... and yes, I *was* interested."

White Friday

Eric laughed. Glenn laughed too, surprising himself. Then he looked at Eric for a few seconds and said, "I'm sorry I hit you."

Eric looked at him and nodded. "I'm sorry I hit you back."

November 26th, Thanksgiving Day... yesterday.

Glenn dreamed. At least, he thought he was dreaming. There were people talking in polite, restrained voices. He could hear them, but not well enough to distinguish what they were saying. He felt vaguely unsettled, as he usually did when sleeping in an unfamiliar place. Not necessarily a bad feeling, just a *not at home* feeling. The bed, of course, was the same type as the one in his bedroom.

A light clicked on nearby. The illumination seeped through his eyelids, and he was finally awake enough to open them. His first sight was Ashley, in her red and grey sweats, moving toward the foot of the bed. Her hair was in a short, messy ponytail. She hadn't used any makeup today. She looked lovely.

She had turned on the small lamp on the nightstand next to the bed. Glenn was laying on top of the sheets, clad in baggy flannel pants and a thick long-sleeved tee— his common winter sleep ensemble. His mouth was dry. He reached toward the nightstand without looking. His fingers wrapped around the sport bottle that they had been sharing. The purple one. It had only a a mouthful of water left; he knocked it back and set the empty bottle back on the stand.

Ashley continued toward the window, pushed open one of the blinds and looked outside. "It's snowing," she said, turning back toward him.

"It's lovely, isn't it?"

"Through a window, yes." She climbed onto the bottom of the bed, crawled up and laid next to him.

"I thought I heard voices."

"Well... that's never a good sign," said the soft voice near his left ear.

"Aside from the usual voices in my head," he said, smiling. He turned his head toward her.

She slid closer and rubbed the tip of her nose against his. "Yeah, I had the TV on for a minute. The weather channel." With that, she snuggled up against his side and draped an arm across his chest.

He put his hand on hers. "What's the forecast?"

"It'll snow for a while."

"Oh... helpful."

"Yeah." He could hear the smile in her voice.

Glenn sighed, content. "That was one of my better naps."

"Mmm. Mine too."

"I could spend the whole weekend like this."

"Mmm-hmm."

He closed his eyes. Maybe they could... maybe they would. He could think of nothing better. Neither of them cared so much about what they were doing or how they looked while doing it or even whether it was especially enjoyable. They cared most about being together. That solitary fact improved everything.

It had been a wonderful Thanksgiving. Yes, he had missed the parade, but they had cooked together and watched football together and, of course, taken their tryptophan-induced nap together. And because he had spent Thanksgiving away from home several years in a row, he had missed that 'home for the holiday' feeling... until now. It was back. He had found it again... or it had found him. Either way, he had felt it today, and it wasn't the food. It wasn't the football. It wasn't even the snow. He was home for the holiday, with Ashley.

They hadn't yet officially declared their relationship, and Glenn didn't care. The relationship existed just fine without a label. They saw each other daily. They kept in touch throughout each day and talked about everything. They hugged and cuddled and had, on two occasions, briefly kissed. She was timid, and she had told him why. He had *seen* why.

"It would be nice," she said softly. "I just think it'd be too much, too fast.

"Mmm," said Glenn. He was, really, not sure how he felt about taking it slow. But he was content, here, with her, and that was something.

"Spending a night together is a big step... even if we do keep our clothes on."

"You're right," he said. "This isn't a race. I'll be ready to step forward when you are." He already felt at home with her. He didn't need to do *this thing* or *that thing* with her to make it better. It would come, as they became more familiar with each other and developed trust.

"I'd like to step forward. I just need to get my shoes on first. You know?"

"You'd be more comfortable without them," he said in a playful tone.

"I went out without shoes. I wasn't afraid. I thought I'd just feel cool grass under my feet. For a while, I did. Then I stepped on something hard and sharp and... it sliced me up real good. So... I guess that's why people wear shoes."

Glenn rolled toward her and pulled her close—slowly but steadily—and she did not resist. He kissed her and she kissed back. He pulled away after a few seconds and looked her in the eyes. "Don't worry. I'm not going anywhere."

She looked up at him and smiled. "Neither am I." She rubbed her nose against his again. "I am going to do some reading, though. Okay?"

"Yeah." He *was* okay with it. He had wanted a relationship with Ashley and now he had it. They were together. When you feel like you've finally come home after years of wandering, there is no need to rush; you can take off your shoes and relax. "I could do some studying, too." He sat up. "I probably won't, though."

"Tomorrow."

"Hmm, maybe."

"I mean, tomorrow, if there's good snow, maybe we can... you know... play in it."

He swung his legs over the side, got up and turned toward her. "Huh. Play in the snow... how come I never thought of that?"

She was crawling toward the edge of the bed. "Maybe because you take it for granted, dear. We don't get much snow where I'm from."

"Oh, come on. I'm sure Alabama is a frozen wasteland in the winter..."

She smacked him on the shoulder. He had probably earned it.

Black Friday, the Friday after Thanksgiving, came to an end. The police and EMTs and firefighters finished their business halfway through the night and were gone. The snow stopped falling around the same time.

Glenn slept. And when he woke up, things were different.

ABOUT THE AUTHOR

Ray Jordan loves God and lives in central Pennsylvania. He enjoys sports, cooking, and epic movies. Also, he could really go for a good turkey pot pie right about now.

Made in the USA
Charleston, SC
21 July 2014